A Marriage Below Zero

A
MARRIAGE
BELOW ZERO

A Novel by Alan Dale

Edited with an Introduction by

Matthew Kaiser
Harvard University

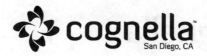

cognella™
San Diego, CA

15 14 13 12 11   1 2 3 4 5

Printed in the United States of America

ISBN: 978-1-609279-57-8

 cognella™

www.cognella.com 800.200.3908

Contents

EDITOR'S INTRODUCTION

I N 1889, New York publishing house G.W. Dillingham had high hopes for their latest paperback, *A Marriage Below Zero*, a "sensation novel" in the tradition of Wilkie Collins's *The Woman in White* (1860) and Mary Elizabeth Braddon's *Lady Audley's Secret* (1862). Sensation novels were plot-driven Victorian thrillers set in that most dangerous and mysterious of locales: the middle-class home. Forget those foggy London streets, or that cliff-top Gothic castle. Parlors, bedrooms, and suburban gardens were the new crime scenes. No longer a refuge from life's horrors, the home was their very source. Ripping the mask from domesticity, sensation novels titillated audiences with accounts of family secrets, double lives, bigamy, adultery, domestic violence, drug abuse, illegitimate children, murderous spouses, in short, with the sordid under-belly of middle-class respectability. In these tales of surveillance, men and women acted as private detectives in their own homes, spying on spouses, parents, servants, and children, who, in turn, spied on them, searching for clues, the slightest trace of abnormality.

Writing under the pseudonym "Alan Dale," drama critic and novelist Alfred J. Cohen attempted in *A Marriage Below Zero* to up the ante in the "sensation" game by shining a light on a phenomenon that had been explored only obliquely or cryptically in English-language novels. Dale's subject was homosexuality. Less constrained by censorship laws than their British counterparts, editors at Dillingham sensed they had a bestseller on their hands. *A Marriage Below Zero* is the first novel in English to depict in unambiguous terms a male homosexual relationship. Narrated from the point of view of a neglected and jealous wife, *A Marriage Below Zero* is a tragicomic account of a clueless young woman's disastrous decision to marry a pretty bachelor, a man whom everyone but the woman herself intuits (or at least suspects) is sexually attracted to men. To the disdain of London socialites, Arthur Ravener seldom appears in public without his male companion, Jack Dillington, a misogynous military officer ten years his senior. With Hellenistic insinuation, West-Enders dub the male couple "Damon and Pythias." *A Marriage Below Zero* is a novel about open secrets, a frigid marriage, erotic miscommunication, about the paradoxical nature of sexual consciousness at the end of the nineteenth century. On the one hand, society has become increasingly knowledgeable about sex, priding itself on detecting its subtle "truth," grasping its nuances and complexities; on the other hand, that same society is blinded by its own sense of moral superiority, its naïve belief in the wholesome stories it tells itself about itself. Like the society it describes, *A Marriage Below Zero* views homosexuality—and sex more generally—with a contradictory mix of urbanity and paranoia. Dale's clueless young heroine is both a victim and a buffoon. A neurotic novel about neurosis, *A Marriage Below Zero* struggles to make sense of the very sexual paradox of which it is a symptom. It brims with irony. Indeed, *A Marriage Below Zero* is surprisingly funny: an erotic comedy of errors that ends grotesquely, horrifically, in death. To Dale's disappointment, reviewers, by and large, attacked the novel on moral grounds, recoiling from its subject matter and its inappropriately frivolous tone. For a short time, Dale's reputation suffered. He shifted his energies to other projects, becoming the most famous drama critic in America. As the years passed, this peculiar, groundbreaking novel faded from memory. By the early twentieth century, it was all but forgotten, dismissed as homophobic and overly sensational by the few gay and lesbian intellectuals who remembered it.

Dale's risky choice of subject was motivated primarily by opportunism, by a desire to capitalize on the public's growing curiosity about homosexuality, its fears that latently gay husbands were undermining the institution of marriage from within. There is no evidence to suggest that Dale was same-sex-oriented, though of course his sexual orientation is impossible to verify. Editors at Dillingham initially hoped the controversy generated by *A Marriage Below Zero* would boost sales. Set primarily in London, Dale's novel was certainly timely, for in the late 1880s British authorities—and the newspaper-reading public at large—were experiencing what can only be described as successive waves of collective homosexual panic. Despite the fact that sodomy was still a felony in Great Britain, and despite the fact that those found guilty of the offense were subject, in theory if seldom in practice, to life in prison, governmental efforts to persecute gay people had abated slightly in the mid nineteenth century, the last public execution for homosexuality having taken place in 1836. Sodomy was officially declassified as a capital offense in 1861. The mood shifted in the mid 1880s, however, a result of the increased visibility of gay or "Uranian" men, as they called themselves. In 1885, Parliament passed the draconian Labouchere Amendment to the Criminal Law Amendment Act, which criminalized all non-penetrative sexual contact between men, including ambiguous acts of overly physical homoerotic affection, assigning such activity the vague label "gross indecency." Thus, Section 11 of the Act, as the Labouchere Amendment was officially known, had the effect of criminalizing same-sex desire itself, in addition to intimate homosexual acts. Ten years later, Oscar Wilde would be prosecuted under this same law and sentenced to two years hard labor. Dale's timing could not have been better, or so he thought. In 1889, the year *A Marriage Below Zero* hit shelves, details of the so-called Cleveland Street Scandal were splashed across the pages of English and American newspapers, when police raided an upscale male brothel in central London. Its clientele consisted of aristocrats, prominent professionals, and even—or so rumors flew—Queen Victoria's grandson, Prince Albert Victor. Unfortunately, Dale had misjudged the public's interest in and tolerance for fictional accounts of homosexual lives, even if those lives ended, as they do in *A Marriage Below Zero*, tragically, as punishment for their unconventionality.

Though some reviewers praised Dale for writing an entertaining and edifying tale of modern marriage, most were distressed by his decision to make his ingénue-narrator—the self-declared victim of male homosexuality—a fool. Self-justifying and self-loathing, desperate for male attention one minute, recoiling from it the next, Elsie Bouverie, whose name echoes that of the adulterous heroine in Flaubert's *Madame Bovary* (1856), is a classic female hysteric. She bemoans the frigidity of her husband, pounding on his locked bedroom door like a Richardsonian rake, even as she expresses disgust at public displays of heterosexual affection, rejecting suitor after suitor. No one appears to take her very seriously, in part because she does not seem to know what she wants. Like Emma Bovary, she is an avid reader of bad novels, which have distorted her view of the world. Elsie accuses everyone around her of being a fool or a hypocrite, mocking (in an aside) an overweight woman on a train, harrumphing at a matron's plunging neckline, even as she admits that she herself is the biggest fool of them all. Elsie is the butt of her friends' private jokes. She is an inept heterosexual. Though she presents herself as a spokeswoman for insulted femininity, for besieged domesticity, she begins her narrative by attacking her own mother as a social-climbing fraud. Elsie is an unreliable narrator and an unreliable authority on sex. She is what makes *A Marriage Below Zero* so delightfully complex.

Even as Dale encourages readers to identify with his heroine by presenting her narrative as a confessional *cri de cœur*, he mischievously undermines that identification by making Elsie painfully—comically— slow to discover the truth: a truth so glaring that even the most sheltered reader will discover it five or six chapters into the novel. That the secret of her husband's homosexuality is not nearly so stubborn or so surprising as Elsie repeatedly professes, indeed, that even her maid seems to view her as a bit of a fool, means that her efforts to portray herself as a melodramatic damsel in distress fall—if not exactly on deaf ears, for her story is certainly pitiable—on ears that are more knowing and jaded than her own. Humorous though it may be, Elsie's extreme ignorance alienates readers, who come to view her perspective as flawed, a bit delusional, biased. If *A Marriage Below Zero* fails to provide sufficient moral clarity on the question of homosexuality, as reviewers complained, it is because the couple's frigid marriage is as much a result of Elsie's hysteria as of Arthur's quasi-secret life. Arthur asks Elsie to marry him precisely because he assumes, after listening approvingly to her rants against heterosexual men, that she has no interest in consummating their marriage. He assumes they are on the same page. Elsie's rage at him, then, is displaced anger at herself for not being honest about her sexual needs. Thus, to the consternation of outraged reviewers, Dale equates anti-homosexual political grandstanding—articulated most overtly in the novel by a Bible-thumping preacher in New York City—with female hysteria, with the epistemological unreliability and critical blindness that results from the unholy union of self-righteousness and sexual repression. *A Marriage Below Zero* is a tragicomic novel about the difficulty of achieving critical distance from one's own sexuality, from the objects of one's desire, even as knowledge of sexuality seems to proliferate at a dizzying rate in modern life. Though the novel is not pro-homosexual by any means, nor particularly sympathetic toward same-sex-oriented people, who come across as tortured, furtive, and self-absorbed, Dale's satirical firepower is reserved almost exclusively for the hypocrisy and self-delusion that underlie middle-class married life. Homosexuality is a pretext. Marriage is Dale's true target.

Extensive biographical information about the man called "Alan Dale" is limited. In his novels and theater reviews, Dale presents himself as a witty outsider laughing at the pageant of modern life. He writes with the ironic detachment of the practiced cynic, embracing his marginal status as the source of his insight. By the early twentieth century, he had become the most popular theater critic in the United States, the scourge of New York producers, directors, and managers, who sometimes barred him from their theaters and regularly implored his bosses to fire him. A pioneer in developing a more populist, sarcastic, and gossipy brand of theater review, Dale loathed what he felt were the literary pretentions of mid-Victorian drama critics. Alfred J. Cohen was born in 1861 to an Anglo-Jewish family in Birmingham, England, where the increased visibility and economic clout of the local Jewish community was a growing source of tension between it and Birmingham's Christian majority. Cohen was educated at King Edward's School and later, or so he claimed, at Oxford University, though no evidence exists that he attended the university. In the early 1880s, he worked in London as a stenographer for American journalist Leander Richardson, who brought him to New York City, where Cohen soon made a name for himself as a feisty and ambitious reporter. In the mid 1880s, Cohen took the *nom de plume* "Alan Dale," after the mischievous songster Alan-a-Dale in Robin Hood's merry band of outlaws. He married Carrie Livingston Frost in 1886 and settled down to married life. From 1887 to 1895, Dale worked as drama critic at Joseph Pulitzer's New York *Evening World*, before William Randolph Hearst recruited him as drama critic for the New York *Journal*. By the early twentieth century, Dale's flippant reviews and jaunty articles were appearing nationally in all Hearst newspapers, as well as in *Cosmopolitan*. Dale had become a minor celebrity, a happy curmudgeon, railing, on behalf of commonsensical America, against Shakespeare, Ibsen, and Shaw, against cultural snobbery. Though Dale regularly chastised playwrights for their gratuitous profanity, he also mocked them for their sexual squeamishness, their prudish or overly dramatic representations of human sexuality. Dale viewed life as an amusing spectacle, an endless parade of bad actors, which he critiqued from his free aisle seat. In addition to his various novels, which included *Jonathan's Home* (1885), *An Eerie He and She* (1890), *My Footlight Husband* (1893), *A Moral Busybody* (1894), *A Girl Who Wrote* (1902), and *When a Man Commutes* (1918), Dale was the author of *Familiar Chats with Queens of the Stage* (1890) and *The Great Wet Way* (1910). Though his attempts at playwriting were less successful, two of his plays enjoyed productions. In 1918, police shut down *The Madonna of the Future*, Dale's comedy about an unmarried woman of means who decides to become a mother, claiming the play was immoral. In 1928, on vacation in England, Dale died of a heart attack on a train headed to his native Birmingham. He was sixty-seven.

Much of Dale's fiction focuses—often to amusing effect—on the seemingly intractable emotional, sexual, and political tensions between modern men and women. Heterosexuality is difficult. Marriage—even a strong one—is no walk in the park. Men and women see each other, Dale suggests, through veils of delusion. Pity them, then, when those veils fall apart. While gender conflict has been a compelling literary theme since time immemorial (some would argue the *most* compelling theme), Dale is one of the first novelists writing in English who had the audacity to declare the obvious: heterosexuality is not for everyone. It leaves some people cold. One of the historically noteworthy aspects of Dale's groundbreaking representation of male homosexuality, an aspect that flies in the face of homophobic stereotypes that persist to this day, is his depiction of gay men as intrinsically—obsessively—relationship-oriented, as bound by a masculine intimacy, a Hellenistic friendship, that no proselytizing maiden can break, no gaggle of disapproving dandies can sever. Arthur Ravener and Jack Dillington are in love. They are inseparable. Dillington pursues Arthur across the Atlantic. They cannot live without each other. Alas, they don't. Of course, jealous Elsie portrays the men's powerful bond as creepy, insinuating that Dillington exerts a Svengali-like influence over young Arthur. In her eyes, their inseparability smacks of addiction more than ardor, servitude more than devotion. The men are nevertheless defined by their union, by their overlapping photographs in one frame, which Elsie discovers at the end of the novel in a paroxysm of hysterical rage. Her paroxysm coincides with her long-anticipated realization, her journey from innocence to experience. Dale's decision to equate male homosexuality with love, with a quasi-public long-term relationship, howsoever threatening to middle-class domesticity that love may be, represents a radical departure from the Victorian convention of portraying gay men as lonely monsters, effeminate clowns, or decadent antisocial rebels. Elsie's vilification of Dillington is understandable. The two are rivals for Arthur's hand. He wins; she loses. Just as Dale humiliates her for her loss, he makes sure to punish Dillington for his victory. Modern sexuality, however, not morality, has the last laugh—it is a bitter, neurotic laugh. Like *A Marriage Below Zero*, sexuality's laughter is sardonic and unsettling.

Matthew Kaiser
Harvard University

A Marriage Below Zero

I seek no sympathies, nor need;
The thorns which I have reaped are of the tree
I planted,—they have torn me,—and I bleed:
I should have known what fruit would spring from such a seed.
 —*Byron*[1]

Soft love, spontaneous tree, its parted root
Must from two hearts with equal vigour shoot;
While each delighted and delighting gives
The pleasing ecstasy which each receives:
Cherish'd with hope, and fed with joy it grows;
Its cheerful buds their opening bloom disclose,
And round the happy soil diffusive odour flows.
If angry fate that mutual care denies,
The fading plant bewails its due supplies;
Wild with despair, or sick with grief, it dies.
 —*Prior*[2]

---

1 *Childe Harold's Pilgrimage* (Canto IV, stanza 10) by George Gordon Byron (1788-1824), English Romantic poet.
2 *Solomon on the Vanity of the World, A Poem* (Book II, 246-255) by Matthew Prior (1664-1721), English poet and diplomat.

INTRODUCTION

I SUPPOSE I am rather frivolous. I believe in the voice of the majority, to a certain extent; and it has announced my giddiness and superficiality so frequently, that there is nothing left for me to do but succumb to this view as pleasantly as possible. I never listen to the minority in any of the social questions with which I am confronted. It would therefore be inconsistent to pay much attention to its estimate of myself.

Butterfly-like I flutter about in society, living in the all sufficient present, reckless of the future, and absolutely declining to recollect the past.

I have a mother who loves me a great deal more than she did some time ago, when I seemed to tacitly insist that she should grow old decently and gracefully. Now I do my best to assist her in her vigorous struggle for perpetual youth, and she is thankful to me; she appreciates my efforts. Ah! it is good to be appreciated, sometimes.

"I really don't know what I should do without you, Elsie," she says, in an occasional outburst of good nature. "You are such a comfort to me; you make me feel as though I were your sister. Sometimes I think I am."

So you see that her affection for me is by no means maternal. I call her "mother" from force of habit, though, accustomed as I am to the word, it often sounds rather ludicrous in my ears.

Conventionality forbids me to use her Christian name. People have always had pronounced prejudices in favor of what they call filial respect, and a quarrel with conventionality is generally fatal, as I have learned. So we trot around to receptions, and kettledrums,[1] and dinners and dances as mother and daughter. I would willingly pass for the former if it were possible to do so, but it is out of the question, unfortunately for dear mamma.

I shall never leave my mother. We shall continue our trot about the social world, until one of us is obliged to give in. I hope I shall be the first to fall, because, like the little boy in the song, I could not play alone. I am convinced that my mother also hopes that she will be the bereaved one. She enjoys life so much, that I cannot blame her.

My demise would necessitate her withdrawal from society for a year or so, but Madame Pauline, in Regent Street, really furnishes such delightful mourning, that, as Mrs. Snooksley Smith said to me the other day: "it is positively a pleasant change to wear it." Mr. Snooksley Smith had been gathered to his fathers a few months previously, so that I know she spoke from experience, poor lonely widow.

I wear a wedding ring. It is concealed beneath a scintillating cluster of diamonds which I have purposely placed on the third finger of my left hand, but it is there. I hate it. It is in the way. If I thought I should ever marry again, I would make it a point of insisting that the lucky man should despise those little golden badges as much as I do.

I must wear mine until I die, I suppose. You see everybody knows that I am Mrs. Ravener; all my friends seem to take an ill-natured delight in emphatically using my married name. I may be as frivolous as I choose, as recklessly flippant as I possibly can, but my wedding ring must remain. It does not upbraid me for my conduct. Not a bit of it. I have a perfect right to do everything in my power to forget it. I would fling my ring to the bottom of the Thames, and still maintain my unquestioned right to

---

1   Parties; the term derives from the English practice of using drums as tables at military fêtes in colonial India.

do so, but,—ah! there is always one of those detestable little conjunctions in the way.

I hope I am making you wonder what all this means, dear reader, because I intend tearing myself away from mamma for a little and devoting some time to you. You say you would not like to inconvenience mamma? Oh, you need not hesitate. I shall tell her that I need a little rest, and shall interpret her surprised "What nonsense, Elsie!" into a motherly injunction to take it. She is still a little afraid of me, you see. She remembers that, like Mr. Bunthorne,[1] I am very terrible when I am thwarted. Though nothing in my behavior nowadays indicates that I have the faintest suspicion of a will of my own, mamma knows better. Perhaps in the solitude of her chamber she wishes that dear Elsie were the sweet little gushing nonentity she appears to be. In time I may make her forget that I have ever been anything else. Perhaps as she grows old (if she ever does) her memory may be dulled. It is just possible that she may pass away in the fond conviction that her only daughter has never crossed her will. Who shall say that I am not charitable?

I am going to write the story of my married life. I intend to open old wounds by confession which, it is popularly said, is good for the soul. The task may do me good. A little taste of bitter recollection can but enhance the value of the sweet vapidity of my present life. I can pause while I am writing, if I feel at all overwhelmed by the flood of reminiscence, which will pour in upon me by the gates which I voluntarily open, to congratulate myself that it is all over forever.

Like the little girl who used to get out of her nice warm bed, and make her sister call out, "There are mice on the floor," so that she might have the pleasure of rushing back again and huddling up under the clothes in an ecstacy of comfort, I will recall the past, in order that I may enjoy the present all the more.

Perhaps that present palls upon me sometimes, though no one guesses it, and I hardly suspect it myself. Possibly it needs all the contrast with the past that I can give it, to render it endurable. I say "possibly" you know. I wish to be consistently frivolous.

---

1   A reference to the poetry-writing buffoon, Reginald Bunthorne, in Gilbert and Sullivan's comic opera *Patience; or, Bunthorne's Bride* (1881), who informs his rival: "Take care. When I am thwarted I am very terrible."

You will be able to remember these remarks when you have read the record of the events which I am about to chronicle, and when you close the book, say with a sigh of relief: "Well, in spite of all, she is living happily ever afterwards."

CHAPTER 1

NO, I shall not weary you with a long account of my childhood, and all that sort of thing. When I read a story, I always skip the pages devoted to a description of the juvenile days of the hero or heroine. They are generally insufferably uninteresting, or interesting only to the writer, and I can find no excuse for selfishness, with such a weapon as a pen in one's hand.

My mother was left a widow when I was a baby. There is a mournful sound about that piece of intelligence, which is absolutely deceptive. In reality it was a most satisfactory outcome of what I was always told was an extremely unhappy marriage. I heard that my father was a charming man, well read, intellectual, courteous and refined. His death was a happy release for both. Poor papa could not tolerate the shallowness of his spouse's hopes and aspirations; while mamma looked upon her husband as an encumbrance, and an obstacle in the way of her social ambition. A husband is very often unnecessary when you are once in the swim of society. When he has given you the protection of his honorable name, and endowed you liberally with the goods of this world, why, the most delicate thing he can then do, is to cease reminding you of these facts, by taking himself off. At least that is the way a great many people look at the matter, I am told.

I was a year old when papa died. What I was there for, I cannot imagine. There was absolutely no reason for my existence. My mother despised children from the bottom of her heart—or, I might more aptly say, the place where her heart was supposed to be. But I thrived on my bottle. I grew disgracefully fat, and outrageously healthy, and it soon became apparent that there would be no difficulty in rearing me. The only person who could have felt any satisfaction at this was my nurse, who, without me to take care of, would have lost a good situation.

I have promised to say little about my childhood, and I will respect my promise.

I was packed off very young to an extremely aristocratic school, where for years dear mamma left me to myself, pursuing her own sweet course in the labyrinthine mazes of society. She paid my bills regularly, and they were pretty big ones, for nothing that could make me subsequently interesting among mamma's dear friends, was neglected. I was to go into society very young. I think she wanted a little excitement, and imagined that she might get some entertainment from a nice, accomplished daughter. Everybody was aware of the fact that she had one, you see, and also cruelly remembered her real age; so why not use the girl to as much advantage as possible? So, I presume she reasoned.

I was "finished" in the most approved manner. I was taught to play the piano with the most provoking persistence, and made day and night hideous with my frenzied interpretations of things in variations, of pyrotechnical morceaux,[1] and of drawing-room "selections."

I sang songs with *roulades*[2] which would have frightened Patti,[3] and effective little *chansons*, with plenty of tra-la-la and tremulo about them. Creatures on whom the education I received would be likely to take effect, ought to be caged up, as dangerous to the community, in my opinion. I spoke villainous French, in order that I might vulgarly interlard my sentences with an occasional Gallic expression. I have done so above. You have Mme. Bobichon, instigated by mamma, to thank for it. A long haired, beery German was going the rounds of the drawing-rooms at this time (I ought to say *salons*, I suppose), and talking the

1   Short musical compositions.
2   Musical embellishments consisting of a rapid run of several notes.
3   Adelina Patti (1843-1919), famous opera soprano.

gullible Londoners into the belief that he was a musical prodigy. I was taught German, I presume, in order that I might be able to tell him, in his own language, how much I adored him. I was very accomplished, in a word—desperately so. I will say this, however: I despised my education. I could see through its superficiality even then.

I enjoyed my school days thoroughly. I liked the society of the merry, laughing, giddy girls I met. Towards the end of my "finishing" period, I went home for a holiday, and the return to school was simply delightful. I dreaded the idea of leaving it for a home which I knew I should detest, and for a mother in whom I had not the faintest interest. At seventeen, however, I was taken into the bosom of my family, and the happiest period of my life came to an abrupt end.

I remained quietly at home for three months before I became that silliest of human beings, a blushing *debutante*. (She doesn't blush long, poor thing.) I had one dear friend whom I regarded as a sister. Letty Bishop had left school two years before I emerged, so that when I was ready to burst upon the social world, she was already a full-fledged society girl.

I shall always remember the ball mamma gave to introduce me to the world. It was a great event for me, an absolute and utter revelation. I rejoiced at the idea of meeting my old school friends, and of resuming the pleasant relations we had enjoyed, without restriction. I was also particularly anxious to become acquainted with members of the male sex, of whom I had heard so much from my friend. I knew none, except John, the butler, who I cannot say impressed me very favorably.

I supposed that men were nice, sensible, jolly beings, immeasurably superior to girls, and with so many more privileges. They could marry whom and when they chose—I thought it, at least—and had unlimited power over creation in general. I hoped in my heart of hearts, that I should soon be chosen, and that some young man would carry me away from mamma to a life which would be more endurable.

As I just said, that ball was an utter revelation to me. I was going to rush at the dear girls I knew, gushingly glad to meet them again after such a long separation, and burningly anxious to take them off to indulge in those nice long talks we had at school.

But when I saw them in my mother's house I hardly recognized them. Could it be possible that these affected, fragile creations, were really the same girls who, only a few months ago, had surreptitiously purchased indigestible cakes, openly read sentimental novels, and enthusiastically sworn eternal friendship the one for the other? Why, they had no eyes for anything female now; all their attentions seemed turned in the direction of the men.

They greeted me with chilling politeness, and turned from me with ill-concealed haste to salute members of the other sex. Of course I had no doubt that they were as eager to meet men as I was. Still, I was not prepared to be treated in this way.

If the behavior of my feminine friends surprised me, I was completely astounded, before the evening was over, at that of the other sex. Why, it was impossible to talk sensibly to these men. They made silly speeches, and showered compliments upon me in a manner that simply caused me consternation and hurt my self respect. I could not imagine what they meant by being so personal. It would have only been after years of familiar intercourse that a girl would have ventured to talk to me as did these men, whom I had never seen before, and with the utmost assurance. It seemed to me that when strangers gave utterance to such ridiculous remarks, they were guilty of nothing less than impertinence.

When they were not unpleasantly self-satisfied, they were absurdly bashful. No girl is ever so contemptuously ill at ease as a bashful man, for whom I have never been able to feel any compassion.

One of our young hereditary legislators asked me to dance, and willing to put him at his ease, for his arms seemed to embarrass him, and his blushes amounted to a positive infirmity, I consented. He seemed to me to be a foolish young peacock, one of those men who Carlyle[1] says attain their maximum of detestability at twenty-five, and ought to be put in a glass case until that period, after which they are supposed to improve. He danced well. I have since learned that most social peacocks do. The poetry of motion seems to accompany lack of brains. When once my lord had disposed of his arm around my waist, he was another being, oh, so much improved!

When the dance was over, he led me into the refreshment room, and brought me an ice. I needed it. I had danced boisterously because I was

---

1   Thomas Carlyle (1795-1881), Scottish essayist, cultural critic, and historian, who viewed the dandy as a symptom of the superficiality of modern life.

young enough to enjoy the exercise for itself alone. I could have passed a much pleasanter time, however, had my partner been my one friend and *confidante*, Letty Bishop, than I had done with the gawky arms of young my lord encircling my waist.

"What a delightful waltz," sighed my lord, as he watched me greedily eating my ice. He was no longer embarrassed, my efforts had been successful.

"Yes," I replied, "I love dancing, and I think you waltz nearly as well as even Miss Bishop, that pretty girl sitting over there."

I pointed to a chair where Letty was reclining, surrounded by, I believe I counted seventeen young men. I thought I had paid him a great compliment. I had enjoyed my dance, and felt in a better humor. My lord did not seem at all elated, however. He became silent, and eyed me sentimentally.

"Why don't you have an ice?" I asked, presently, feeling annoyed at his stupidity. "This pineapple is very good—there are real pieces of fruit in it."

"Ah, Miss Bouverie," said he, "I am not in an ice humor."

"Ha, Ha! what a good pun!" I laughed flippantly, wishing he would remove his eyes. "You ought to keep me in countenance, though. I always think people look so gluttonous eating by themselves."

My lord took a chair and an ice at the same time, and sat down beside me. He spoke very little, which I ascribed to the fact that he was enjoying his ice. When he had finished, he asked me if I had any more dances to give him. I looked at my programme. I had none. My lord scowled.

"Miss Bouverie," he said, "you are the only girl here I care about dancing with. All these belles of sixteen seasons weary me," languidly, "and you give me only one meagre waltz."

"I think you are very rude to my guests," I answered, vexed. "They are nearly all young girls, and most of them are nice ones, too. I would as soon dance with you as with anybody, but as this is my mother's party, I believe I am not allowed to choose. I must take everybody who asks me, I suppose. Not that it matters much, however," I added indifferently. "I can't see that a partner makes much difference as long as he dances well. One has no time to talk."

My lord looked surprised. "You are too young," he said, with what I considered unpardonable frankness. Then in a low tone, "Miss Bouverie,

I am so glad you are now 'out.' I shan't refuse any more invitations. I've been sending refusals to everybody lately, you know."

Lucky people, I thought. I rose in disgust, and left him. I felt sick at heart. I had been dancing all the evening, and all my partners annoyed me. They appeared to imagine that I was a doll, and condescended to play with me. Was that the way men always treated girls, I asked myself? A long time has elapsed since that evening, but though I have since learned that a man who never says a pretty thing, is an abnormal being who will ultimately sink into obscurity, I wonder that it should be so.

I was completely disappointed. Even Letty Bishop seemed to view me with less interest, while the men were around. She had known me longer than she had known them, and surely I ought to have been considered first.

I felt that I could never like the other sex if it were composed exclusively of creatures like those with whom I had danced, under the most favorable circumstances too, namely, in my mother's house. From what I had seen, I judged that in the social world, women must be the sworn enemies of women, and men the everlasting foes of men. Girls I had heard declare themselves to be eternal friends, never spoke to each other during the evening, and I failed to notice a man address a word to one of his own sex, which would indicate any friendly interest in it.

I wept bitterly as I cast aside my fine feathers that night. My self-respect was wounded. Men had treated me as though I were a silly toy, and I had expected so much from them, and had thought they would be even more companionable than women.

Companionable! Great goodness!

You will probably have arrived at the conclusion by this time, dear readers, that I was a fool. If, however, I possessed no peculiarities, I should not venture to be sitting here. Indeed, I suppose I should be a respectable British matron, with half-a-dozen sturdy children, and—let me see, it is ten o'clock—I might now be ordering a boiled leg of mutton with caper sauce for my little olive-branches' dinner.

CHAPTER 2

M ISS Bishop lived in that terribly respectable quarter of London known as Colville Gardens, where the rows of houses look as though they are pining to be allowed a little architectural license, or an escape of some kind from the exhausting restrictions of the prudery in which they have been designed.

Letty was a strange girl, a curious combination of extreme frivolity, shrewd common sense and warm-heartedness. I liked her, because she was the first girl who had ever shown me any kindness. She would listen to my ideas of things with the utmost good temper, point out where she thought I was mistaken, and allow me the luxury of differing from her; which you will admit is a favor usually hard to obtain from friends. Letty Bishop's father was by no means rich. He had been left a widower many years before, and to Letty was assigned the duty of tending his latter years. This she did with a devotion which I admired. I might have emulated her example, but my mother would have shuddered at, and repudiated, the idea of "latter years."

After my miserable failure as a "blushing *debutante*," I was not long in seeking Letty's society. Early the next morning I was in Colville Gardens. I found Letty in the breakfast-room, reading a parliamentary debate in one of the morning papers, so that she could discuss it with her father when he returned from his office. She was attired in the wrapper which women affect nowadays. She threw down her paper when she saw me, and advancing toward me, gave me an effusive kiss on each cheek.

"So glad to see you, dear," she said, "I expected you would be round this morning. Elsie, let me congratulate you on your great success. I'm really proud of you."

I looked what I felt—surprised. That I had been successful, was something I had never contemplated. "I don't know what you mean, Letty," I murmured. "I never spent such a mournfully wretched evening in my life. But," I added, "put on your things and let us go for a nice walk, and I will tell you all about it."

"Now you know, dear," said Letty, sinking into her comfortable chair, "that if there is one thing on the face of this earth which I cordially detest, it is a 'nice walk,' It makes one look so dreadfully healthy, and I abhor dairymaid beauty. No, dear, if you have anything to tell me, say it here, in this cosy room. I'm all ears."

This was not strictly true; Miss Bishop's ears were of the style which our imaginative novelists liken to "dainty pink shells." But I knew what she meant, and was not in a particularly humorous mood, so I took off my things and sat down. "Letty," I said, quietly, "tell me why I was a success."

I felt and looked rather dejected, but she did not appear to notice this.

"Why you were a success," she replied energetically, "because you had more partners than you wanted; because you looked lovely in that dear little white silk dress; because all the men noticed you and asked numerous questions about you, and because—well, my dear, I can't give any more reasons; they are obvious. You must know them as well as I do."

I was disappointed. "Tell me, Letty," I asked, "was this a representative party? Was it an average affair?"

"Far above the average, my dear," was Letty's prompt response. "There was at least a man to every two girls, which is unusual, there being generally about seventeen times as many women as men. Then the men were really very nice. Mrs. Bouverie deserves great credit for her selection. The wallflowers were composed of those who deserved to be wallflowers, which is worth noting. The supper was excellent, the floor good, the music admirable, and the arrangements perfect."

Miss Bishop folded her hands after these dogmatic utterances, and half closing her eyes looked at me through her heavy eyelashes. I fidgetted and was uncomfortable.

"If the selection of men were really good," I said thoughtfully and grammatically, "I never want to see a bad selection. Letty, every one of my partners made fun of me. What I have done I don't know, but a man must think very little of a girl to be constantly telling her that her cheeks are like roses, her eyes like stars, her lips—Ah; I sicken when I think of it. Do you mean to say that men talk like that to girls whom they really like and respect?" I was half crying.

Letty rose and kissed me. "You are an innocent little thing," she said, with plaintive condescension, "and my dear,"—quite cheerfully—"I am afraid you are going to have plenty of trouble. Why, I assure you, that a man who doesn't say pretty things to girls is looked upon as a man who can't say them—that is, a boor. Men who talk sense—and there are very, very few of them,—are considered egotistical nuisances. Once I had a partner who had traveled considerably, and he would insist upon describing his travels. He used to carry me off to the Red Sea, lead me gently to the desert of Sahara, or row me tenderly over the lakes of Switzerland. He was very wearisome. I hated him. Yes, Elsie, dear," she went on, seeming positively to enjoy my look of disgust, "I would sooner any day hear something about my pretty eyes and my peach-like cheeks, than a graphic description of the Saharan desert, in a ball-room."

My best friend was leaving me alone and a feeling of desolation came over me. "Can't men talk with girls as they would with men?" I asked. "It seems to me that they must take us for very inferior beings. Men surely don't pay each other idiotic compliments, do they?"

Letty grew serious, and a faint blush deepened the "peach-like" color to which she had already referred. "What men say to one another," she remarked, "I am afraid our ears would hardly tolerate. When my brother Ralph was at home—before he went to China—we always used to have the house full of young fellows. I used frequently to come upon them, when they were laughing heartily, and evidently enjoying themselves. I wanted to laugh as well, but they invariably stopped when they saw me, as though I were a wet blanket. Once or twice I asked them to tell me what was amusing them. The youngest of the party blushed, while the oldest adroitly changed the subject. I presume," said Letty, with charming resignation, "that they were afraid of shocking me. I didn't think so then, but I do now. Men like their little jokes, but—I am afraid we shouldn't."

"I wish mamma would let society alone," I pouted sullenly, feeling thoroughly ill-tempered. "I know I shall be forced to flutter about drawing-rooms until one of these men wants my star-like eyes and my satin complexion for his own. I don't look forward to much happiness. I'd sooner be a governess, or a shorthand writer, or—or—anything." I ended in a burst of indignation.

Miss Bishop laughed, and then became thoughtful. "Elsie," she said presently, "have you ever met Arthur Ravener and Captain Jack Dillington?"

"No," I said shortly, "and I'm not particularly anxious to do so."

"Arthur Ravener and Captain Jack Dillington," pursued Letty, disdaining to notice my petulance, "are known in society as Damon and Pythias.[1] They are inseparable. Such a case of friendship I have never seen. I half expected they would be at your mother's party, but I presume they were not invited. I have never met one without the other. They always enter a ball-room together and leave together. Of course they can't dance with each other, but I'm sure they regret that fact. They are together between the dances, conversing with as much zest as though they had not met for a month. Girls don't like them because they talk downright, painful sense. Men seem to despise them. You might appreciate them, however," with a smile.

"I'm sure I should," I said, enthusiastically. "Men who are capable of feeling deep friendship cannot be fools. I should like to know them,

---

1   Symbols of undying friendship between men, Damon and Pythias were Pythagorean philosophers from the fourth century BCE. Condemned to death for treason by the tyrant Dionysus I of Syracuse, Pythias, according to legend, begs to return to Greece before his execution to settle his affairs. Dionysus agrees on condition that Pythias's friend Damon remain in Syracuse in his place, acting as human collateral, subject to execution in the event Pythias flees. When Pythias returns on schedule, Dionysus is so touched by his loyalty to his friend, that he issues a pardon and makes the two men his court philosophers.

Letty. As long as I have to be a society butterfly, I may as well make myself as comfortable as I can under the circumstances."

"You're a strange girl," remarked Letty, with a sigh, "but," reflectively, "I suppose you can't help it. The next opportunity I have I will introduce you to Arthur Ravener. I can promise you he will pay you no compliments. He'll talk books or politics or—anything unseasonable."

"Or Captain Jack Dillington?" I suggested.

"They rarely speak of one another," said Miss Bishop. "Why, I don't know. Some people call them mysteries, because they can't understand them; but—you shall judge for yourself."

"Thank you, Letty," I said, gratefully, and I brought my visit to a close.

Perhaps as I walked home slowly, I may have indulged in a little complacent recognition of my own superiority. I had a soul above social shallowness, I told myself, and it was hardly likely that I should ever be happy in my home surroundings. I know now that it is one of the laws of nature that a budding woman should rejoice in the admiration of the other sex, should court its favor, and should be plunged into dire misery if she find it not. I must have been a peculiar girl, I suppose. Peculiarities do not always bring undiluted happiness to their owners. I paid dearly for mine, and the debt is not yet liquidated.

CHAPTER 3

F OUR weeks later, after a weary round of festivities (so called), I was sitting discontentedly in Lady Burlington's tawdry drawing-room, wondering why it was that the time passed so slowly. Miss Angelina Fotheringay was singing "*Voi che sapete,*"[1] with a hideous Italian accent, and in a gratingly harsh voice. When she began I was anxious to see how she would conduct herself with regard to the high notes in the song, and was prepared to respect her if she would calmly and delicately evade them. Such a proceeding, however, was evidently far from her intentions. She went over them neck and crop, landing in the midst of a heart-rending shriek, but placidly pursuing her course uninjured. My nerves were shocked. I had an ear for music and was therefore clearly out of place.

I wonder why girls will sing Italian and French songs which they cannot pronounce, when there are so many pretty English ballads which are within their scope. French people laugh at our rendering of their songs, and make most unflattering allusions to our efforts. They

---

1 Famous aria, "You, who know [what love is]," from Mozart's *The Marriage of Figaro* (1786).

have a right to make these allusions. You will very rarely, if ever, hear a Frenchwoman attack an English song. She prefers a field in which she knows she will be at home.

"Thanks, so much, dear," I heard Lady Burlington bleat as the songstress concluded amid a volley of applause. I applauded, too, because I was glad the song was at an end.

"I know I am dreadfully importunate," continued my hostess, "but won't you give us one more song? It is such a treat to hear you. Do, dear," pursued Lady Burlington, as Angelina became coy. "There's that pretty little thing you sing so sweetly, let me see—what is it? Ah, I remember 'Angels ever bright and fair.' "[1]

"Angels ever bright and fair," a pretty little thing! Ye gods!

Miss Fotheringay sat down at the piano again, and having hooked a vapid-looking youth to turn over the pages for her, proceeded to request those unhappy angels to take, oh, take her to their care. She concluded with an operatic flourish, and then without being asked favored the company with a little something in variations, of which I shall never know the name.

I felt positively ill, and when Lady Burlington requested me to play, pettishly declined. As I have already said I had a stock of drawing-room pieces which my fashionable professor had selected; but I hated them. I was thoroughly cross, and longed for something or somebody to distract my mind.

No sooner had I expressed this longing to myself than I noticed two young men enter the drawing-room. They attracted my attention at once. The younger was a tall, slightly built man, about twenty-five years of age. His features were so regular, and his complexion so perfect, that if you had shaven off the small golden moustache which adorned his upper lip, and dressed him in my garments, I felt that he would have done them much more credit than I could ever hope to do. He was extremely pretty. His clothes were faultless, his light hair was carefully brushed, and his appearance altogether irreproachable.

I cannot say as much for his companion, who must have been some ten years his senior. This gentleman had a puffy face, with thick red lips,

---

1   From Georg Friedrich Händel's tragic oratorio *Theodora* (1749), which concerns Christian martyrdom.

and beady black eyes, something like those of a canary, but not as clear. He had the most unpleasant looking mouth I have ever seen, and as he wore no moustache whatever, it was very visible.

The two new arrivals sat down together during the progress of a song. Then they made their greetings in a quietly dignified manner, and were soon separated in the crowd. I noticed that the younger man looked continually after his friend when the latter went his way. I was still wondering who the two gentlemen were, when I saw Letty Bishop energetically steering her way in my direction, followed closely by the younger.

"Ah, I've been looking for you, Elsie," she said impulsively, regardless of etiquette. "I want to introduce you to Mr. Arthur Ravener. My friend, Miss Bouverie, Mr. Ravener."

Mr. Ravener took the vacant seat beside me, and on closer inspection I found his complexion quite as perfect and his features quite as regular as they had seemed when there was distance between us.

"You do not appear to be enjoying yourself, Miss Bouverie," he said in soft, musical tones.[1]

"I am not indeed," I answered, vexed that he had been able to read my feelings so easily, "I think musical evenings are detestable."

"Query: Is this a musical evening?" Mr. Ravener sank his voice to a whisper, and I laughed outright. The ice was broken.

We entered upon a conversation which was thoroughly delightful, to me at any rate. I found that Arthur Ravener was fond of music, and understood it thoroughly. He asked who were my favorite composers. I told him that I had never been allowed to have any favorites. I had been dosed with Brinley Richards, Sydney Smith and Kuhe,[2] and the effect had been extremely injurious. I liked to hear classical music. It did not weary me in the least; in fact, if I had been properly educated, I might have proved a fairly competent musician.

---

1   In late-Victorian gay or "Uranian" subculture, "being musical" euphemistically referred to "being same-sex oriented."

2   Henry Brinley Richards (1817-1885), Welsh composer; Sydney Smith (1839-1889), English pianist and composer; Wilhelm Kuhe (1823-1912), German pianist and composer.

He was drawing me out, actually. I had not said as much since I left school to any new acquaintance. Here I was talking to a man with as much ease as though he were one of my beloved feminine school-friends. Mr. Ravener listened to me very attentively. He interposed soft "Oh, indeeds," and "Ah's" in a very pleasant manner, and appeared to be interested. He was very serious and extremely deferential. His face showed none of the changes that steal involuntarily over the features of most men when they speak to young girls. He talked to me as unconcernedly as though I were a man. I became as confidential as though he were a woman. I said presently, "if you are so fond of music, how is it you come to evenings like this?"

"May I address the same question to you?" he asked.

"Oh, that's another thing," I replied. "Girls can't do as they like, you know. They have to follow in the paths their fathers and mothers make for them. But I should have thought it would have been different with men."

"It is not, however," said Mr. Ravener, quietly, and I suppose he thought that settled it, as he dropped the subject. I noticed that he seemed to be eagerly searching for some one in the crowd, and at last I saw his eyes rest upon his unprepossessing friend.

"Are you afraid your friend is not enjoying himself?" I asked, rather cheekily I admit.

He reddened slightly. "Captain Dillington always enjoys himself," he said quietly. "He is very happy in society."

I remembered Letty's story of Damon and Pythias, and longed to know something of these two young men, one of whom at least was different from the ordinary drawing-room specimen. Arthur Ravener was certainly attractive, and I felt I was going to be interested in him, so I must be excused if I showed too much curiosity.

"How rarely you find two really sincere friends," I remarked, rather sentimentally. "The present time seems to be wonderfully unsuited to such a tie."

"That is true"—very laconically.

"I think there is nothing so beautiful as friendship," I went on, with persistence.

"You have heard of Damon and Pythias," he said quickly, reading me like a book. I blushed deeply and was then furiously angry with myself. "I don't mind," he went on. "Make all the fun of us you like."

"Mr. Ravener," I protested, "I assure you that when I heard of the friendship existing between you and Captain Dillington, I became interested in you." (A pretty little declaration to make.) "I don't see where any fun comes in. I am tired of the stupid men I meet at such gatherings as these. They have not enough feeling about their composition to allow them to make friends. Far from feeling amused at Damon and Pythias, I am deeply interested in them."

Arthur Ravener looked pleased. I went on gushing like the school-girl I was. "I can think a great deal better of a young man who is capable of being sincerely attached to a companion, than I can of those foolish chatterboxes over there, who are forever telling me I have pretty eyes, pretty hair and a pretty figure, as though I had not been intimately acquainted with myself for the last seventeen years. Don't think I laugh at you, Mr. Ravener, I am very much interested." Then, so ingenuously that it could hardly be considered rude, "I should like to hear all about Captain Dillington, and how you came to know him?"

"There surely can be nothing to tell," he said in strained tones. "What is the friendship between two young men that you should deem it worth discussing?"

"It is worth discussing," I impulsively asserted. "What are we going to talk about? You are not going to tell me about my sylph-like form, or compare my charms with those of my less fortunate friends?"

"No," he replied gravely, "you will find that is not my style when you know me better. I trust we shall know each other better, Miss Bouverie," he remarked quietly.

"Yes." I blushed in my prettiest manner, and cast my eyes down. I was determined to impress Arthur Ravener favorably. I looked extremely well when my long fringed lids could be seen advantageously. Picture my disgust and annoyance when, looking up again, I found I was alone, and just in time to see Arthur Ravener vanishing from the room with Captain Dillington. Even my acquiescence in his wish for our better acquaintance had not been sufficiently interesting to keep him at my side.

He was gone. "Well," I said to myself, "the claims of friendship are great. He is not very polite, but let him go"—which was extremely kind of me, as he had already gone.

Later in the evening I saw the two young men again. Arthur Ravener did not approach me, but bowed in an astonishingly friendly manner, and I, anxious not to seem piqued, returned the nod, accompanied by a smile.

I was subsequently made acquainted with Captain Dillington, for whom, after I had been in his society five minutes, I felt an overwhelming dislike. I cannot say what it was that induced the impression, but Captain Dillington reminded me of a toad, from his beady little eyes, to his sleek, smooth shaven face. He was conspicuously and effusively polite, which I always consider an unpleasant feature in any man's behavior. Though he paid me no compliments, I was uneasy in his society; again I say I do not know why. We discussed various subjects; he in his oily, complacent manner, I in my superficial, gushing way. I was delighted when he left me, but I could not recover my previous serenity.

It was now the hour when departures were expected with resignation; in fact, Lady Burlington was yawning most openly—if I were in a flippant mood, I should consider that a tolerably decent pun—and I could see the poor thing thought she had entertained us sufficiently.

"Good-night, dear Lady Burlington," I said affectionately, with a smile which mamma would have given six years of her life to see; "I have spent a delightful evening."

May I be forgiven that sin, and the thousands of others of a like nature which I have committed, rebelling as I have rebelled against their absurdity. May all who sin in a like manner be forgiven. May only society that knows these words are mostly sins, and that yet accepts them, be unforgiven! That is what I wish.

"How did you like them?" asked Letty Bishop, as I stood in the hall being cloaked, while I silently vowed to myself that I would tell no more lies to my hostesses.

"Who's them?" I inquired ungrammatically and peevishly, for I was tired.

"Arthur Ravener and Captain Dillington."

"I don't know," I answered. "Mr. Ravener was away from me before I could make up my mind whether I liked him or not. I forgive him freely."

"Ah!" said Letty, with such detestable unction that, friend though I was, I could have enjoyed boxing her ears, "he doesn't pay you compliments. I expect the amiability was all on your side."

I made no answer, but with a hasty "good-night," I jumped into the carriage which was awaiting me and was borne homewards.

CHAPTER 4

ARTHUR Ravener called to "see mamma" a few days later, at least that was the nominal object of his visit, I believe. There is a great deal of humbug about us Londoners. In America young men when they are slightly smitten call upon a girl openly and without beating about the bush; here they ask to see the papas, and the mammas, and the brothers, and the duennas,[1] and everybody but the person they really want.

The idea of any young man deliberately calling to see mamma was so ludicrous, that when I heard of it I laughed. I knew he had come to see me, and I should have thought all the more of him if he had admitted the fact like a man. I was studying hard when I heard him go into the library. I was not puzzling over mathematics, or physics, but was extremely engrossed in a cook-book. I had made a tart, the crust of which was so hideously and irrepressibly solid, that when I had tried to insert a knife in it, the contents of the plate had flown ceilingwards, and cook had looked at me sardonically happy. I hated the woman for that look. I went into the library with a little dab of jam on my cheek, and I was too lazy to worry about it. It was a big room, filled with exquisitely bound

---

1   Chaperones.

books. Dear mamma was very anxious that every volume should be beautifully leather-covered. The contents of the covers were a secondary consideration. It was the correct thing to have a library. It was a good place into which to usher people.

"I thought I would just run in to see if you had recovered from your fatigue of the other night," he said, after we had exchanged salutations.

"Is that why you wished to see mamma?" I asked demurely.

"Of course," he answered. "Mrs. Bouverie might prefer to give me the information herself."

"She couldn't," I declared rather boisterously, "for the simple reason that she never knew that I was fatigued. As a matter of fact I was not, I was bored. The only pleasant part of the evening was furnished by you. There is a compliment for you, before you have been in the house five minutes."

I was very lively indeed, but the arrival of mamma dampened my ardor. She sailed into the room, and seemed extremely pleased to see Mr. Ravener. She liked young men, and always treated them graciously. She did not stay long, however, but begged to be excused. Some girls might have considered this a delicate and motherly piece of consideration. I did not. I had nothing to say to Arthur Ravener or any other young man that might not have been published in the daily papers if the editors had seen fit to inflict it upon their readers. He took one arm chair and I sat opposite. I did not feel at all called upon to talk about the weather and other pleasantly conventional topics. Mr. Ravener had certainly made a most favorable impression upon my maidenly heart.

"You are all over jam, Miss Bouverie," he remarked, as I sat down.

"Don't remind me of my troubles," said I, "I have been cooking very unsuccessfully, and I feel miserable. By the bye, pardon my rudeness in forgetting to ask after the health of Captain Dillington."

There had been a smile on his face as I began my speech. It froze at once—as they say in the novels. A pained blush spread itself slowly over his face. "Captain Dillington," he said deliberately, "is well. Why are you so interested in him?"

"Only because you are," I replied flippantly. "It is the mutual attachment of you two young men that interests me. I think I told you so before, Mr. Ravener."

There was silence for a long time. It was not an eloquent silence. I employed a few leisure moments in removing the jam from my face. He bit his small moustache, as young men often do, more I believe to show that they have one to bite, than because they like it.

"Miss Bouverie," said Arthur Ravener, "you say you were interested in me because you found that I did not pay you silly compliments and talk nonsense. Now don't think me impertinent, if I tell you that I rejoice in the fact that I have met somebody who does not care for such nonsense. Perhaps you will like it better when you are older"—regretfully.

"Never," said I. All the jam was now removed, and though I felt sticky, no one could guess that fact.

"Do you think a young man and woman ought to converse as though they were brother and sister—platonically, I mean?"

"Mr. Ravener," said I, pettishly, "I do not intend to talk metaphysics with you. I have ideas of my own. I like a man, if I have to meet him often, to talk sense."

"Suppose you fell in love?"—tentatively.

"Yes," said I, trying hard to blush a little and failing in a most abject manner. "You are rather impertinent, Mr. Ravener, but no matter. If I ever fell in love, I should see no necessity for discussing it with my 'loved one.' I should not like him any better if he deared and darlinged me. I think I should despise him. I know some people must be demonstrative. Letty Bishop kisses her father about sixteen times in the course of an evening. I suppose she likes it, but it always seems to me very unnecessary. I cannot imagine myself kissing mamma, even if—even if—" I hesitated.

"Even if what?" he asked, unpardonably interested.

"Never mind," sharply. "I was going to reveal family matters to a stranger. You are a stranger, you know. I was going to say—don't think me awful—that I cannot imagine myself kissing mamma even if she did not powder."

He looked rather shocked at my frankness, and I respected him for it. He did not smile, and I went back to my theme. "I could not be demonstrative," I declared. "It seems to me so dreadfully coarse. I flatter myself that I am extremely matter-of-fact."

"I thought so," he said, "and so did—" He stopped in some slight confusion, and reddened in that most provoking manner that people have.

"So did who?" I asked.

"I was merely going to say—"

"Mr. Ravener," I said deliberately. "I want to know who else thought as you did about me."

I suppose he saw I was somewhat determined. "Captain Dillington," he answered in a low tone.

I was thoroughly displeased, and most unreasonably so. Only a few moments previously there was I declaring that the intense friendship of these two young men was something I admired. Now I felt vexed because these boon companions should discuss a girl in whom one of them confessed that he was interested. Men are right when they say one should never expect logic from a woman. I place myself at the head of the unreasonable list.

"You are vexed?" he asked, really troubled.

"Not a bit," promptly. Women cannot reason, but no one can beat them at fibbing. (Fibbing is a polite word for it.)

He seemed relieved. "Do you know, Miss Bouverie," he said as he rose to go, "I can talk to you, as I can to no other girl. That is a positive fact. I don't feel that the instant I leave you, you will run to some feminine bosom and dissect me."

"I shouldn't care enough about you to do that," I said rudely. Could anything have been more impolite? If he could have done anything to increase the good impression he had made upon me, he did it then by simply laughing in a hearty, boyish manner, without an atom of vexation apparent. I had used words of the same purport to partners at some of the hateful parties I had attended, and had been greeted with "Cruel Miss Bouverie"; "Oh, Miss Bouverie, you do not mean it"; "You treat me very badly, Miss Bouverie."

How they annoyed me, those men. I must confess that Arthur Ravener was rapidly becoming more than interesting. Frankness is one of my characteristics.

CHAPTER 5

I FIRMLY believe that if I had told mamma that the Grand Mogul was coming to dinner, and that the Mikado of Japan intended dropping in during the evening in a friendly way, she would simply have remarked, "I am pleased to hear it; we must entertain them." Arthur Ravener's frequent appearance at our house caused not the least surprise, and interested her but slightly. "He is a nice young fellow, Elsie," she said on one occasion. "He is very attentive to you, of course, but there is something about him I don't quite understand. He is cold and undemonstrative, and yet I can tell that he likes you. He seems to have something on his mind."

"Well, that is better than not possessing a mind to have anything on," I retorted in my unpleasantly pert way, "as is the case with the usual nonentities of society."

"Elsie," said my mother, "I dislike to hear a young girl like yourself belittle the people you are accustomed to meet. You may be far superior to them, but—excuse me—I doubt it."

I was snubbed and subsided.

One afternoon as I was walking down Oxford Street, I saw Arthur Ravener and Captain Dillington approaching. Only the latter noticed me at first. He nudged Arthur and, with an indescribably ugly smile on his face, said something to him. I longed to know what it was, woman-like, because I instinctively felt it was not for my ears. Arthur reddened in a most uncomfortable way, and Captain Dillington laughed. I felt annoyed. I resolved that they should stop and speak to me, though I am sure they had no intention of so doing. Accordingly when they raised their hats, by a dainty little feminine manœuvre, I contrived to make them stop. Captain Dillington greeted me boldly. Arthur Ravener seemed tongue-tied.

"Why do you never come to see us, Captain Dillington?" I asked in my airy way, as they turned and walked back with me.

"Would you care to have us both, Miss Bouverie?"

"I don't see why not. There is plenty of room for you."

"I wonder if you will always be as accommodating, Miss Bouverie?" There was something so insolent in his tone, that I became scarlet in the face. I cannot explain what there was offensive in his speech. You who read it will say that I made a mountain out of a molehill. It impressed Arthur Ravener as it impressed me.

"Take care, Dillington," I heard him say in a low voice, as I turned towards a shop window to cool down.

"If you care to come, Captain Dillington," I said haughtily, "we shall be pleased. If you do not care to come—" I shrugged my shoulders; that is very expressive.

The Captain looked alarmed. "I assure you, Miss Bouverie," he said, "you misunderstood me. I should be delighted to call. I am not at all bashful. I feel convinced that we shall meet a great deal"—he made a marked pause—"later."

I cannot describe the look on Arthur Ravener's face. I feel that novelists would call it "the look of the hunted antelope brought to bay." I have no doubt their simile is a good one, though I have never seen an antelope hunted or otherwise.

"Captain Dillington pays very few visits," said Arthur Ravener, lamely. "He sees very little society, indeed."

"Except yours," remarked the Captain.

"Except mine," echoed Arthur, slowly. "But, Captain," appealingly, "I should like you to call one day this week upon Mrs. Bouverie; I think you could manage it if you tried, couldn't you?"

Captain Dillington nodded, and I, not at all anxious to prolong the scene, skipped into a shop with a hasty "good afternoon."

I confess I was puzzled. What Arthur Ravener could see to admire in Captain Dillington it was utterly impossible for me to divine. That the tie which held them together was strong and binding, I could not for a moment doubt. I have always heard that dissimilar spirits form friendships of long duration, but I could not realize that this would hold good in the case of Arthur Ravener and Captain Dillington, one an apparently frank young man who could only just have "begun to live," the other a repulsive being, with no particularly redeeming feature.

I had already seen them often together, and I knew Arthur Ravener was a different man when removed from his friend. It was not true that Captain Dillington saw but little society. He accompanied Arthur on all occasions. In fact, I had never met the one without the other, except at home. Captain Dillington was the chaperon, or at least I looked upon him in that light. However, excuses will never stand analysis.

"What are you doing in here, Elsie?"

I turned round, and beheld Letty Bishop laden with parcels.

"I came in here to look at some—" I began to stammer hopelessly. I never could fib successfully when taken by surprise, which shows that I was an amateur in the art.

Miss Bishop opened the door and looked down the street. Of course she saw the retreating forms of Damon and Pythias, as she called them.

"No, dear," she said calmly, "you came in here to look at nothing at all. You wanted to avoid a certain couple I see fading in the distance. Are you going home, Elsie?"

Yes, I was going home. I admitted the fact. We stepped out into the noise of Oxford Street.

"Elsie," said Letty, suddenly, "I want to talk to you seriously on a subject upon which—pardon me, my dear—I am afraid your mother will have but little to say. You and I have always been great friends, have we not, dear?"

I hate any one to be affecting, especially in the street. I had an awful idea that there was pathos in Miss Bishop's voice, but I made a vow that nothing should induce me to weep and redden my nose, no matter how harrowing she became.

"Yes," I said, "we've been great friends, Letty, and as neither of us intend shuffling off just yet, I vote that we go on being friends, and say nothing about it."

"You can be as flippant as you like," said Miss Bishop severely, "but I am going to talk to you just the same. You remember, Elsie, at the beginning of the season, how miserable you were at all the festivities, and how you dreaded the silly men, as you called them, whom you were obliged to meet. I told you of Damon and Pythias. I introduced you to Arthur Ravener."

"Well?"—impatiently.

"I never imagined that the introduction would lead to anything."

"No?" I was really boiling over with rage, but I tried to conceal that fact.

"No. But it has. People are coupling your name with that of Arthur Ravener. No, don't interrupt me. If I did not care for you, I should say nothing. Look here, Elsie. I am quite certain that you will never be happy, if you do anything rashly. Arthur Ravener is very unpopular. The men won't look at him. I was speaking to my cousin Ned about him the other day, since I have noticed how you encouraged him."

"I—"

"— and Ned told me to warn any friend of mine against him. Why? I asked. He would give me no reason, but, my dear, Ned is a conservative old fellow, and you so rarely hear him say a bad word against anybody, that if he does make an attack it carries weight with it. Personally, I like Ravener; but, my dear, I cannot help listening to what people say. Why I heard the remark the other day that the only reason Ravener and Dillington went into society at all, was to borrow its cloak of respectability."

"Perhaps you think they are highway robbers in disguise, or forgers, or playful assassins?"

"I think nothing, my dear. I only tell you what people say. I do that merely because it was I who introduced you. I had no more idea that you and Arthur Ravener would ever care for one another—"

"Did I say I cared for Arthur Ravener?"

"No, but you do, and my prophetic soul tells me that you will throw yourself away upon him."

"Don't listen to what people say, my child," I remarked loftily, "and you will be a great deal happier. Since you have been talking I have come to the conclusion that I like Arthur Ravener immensely. When I marry it will not be for the sake of my lovely society friends—but for my own. You have done your duty, my dear. You have warned me against a young man of whom you know positively nothing. Thanks. If I can return the compliment at any time, command me."

Then, thinking I could not improve upon this cutting rejoinder, I tripped away.

CHAPTER 6

N O one who has followed me thus far can accuse me of having tried to make myself attractive to my readers. My later experiences have taught me that girls who despise what are generally acknowledged to be the pleasures of girlhood, will get but little sympathy in this world. Perhaps that is as it should be. I must have been eccentric.

I remember that I once heard a young man who had been dancing with a corsetless maiden, a believer in the laws of health, declare that such girls ought not to be allowed in a ball-room. To be accepted by society, you must follow the laws it prescribes. The right to be eccentric must be earned—and it takes time to earn it. What right had a chit like myself to declare that I found the young men whom I was called upon to meet, undesirable and uninteresting? Who put such ideas into my head? I cannot lay the blame upon anybody. The ideas were there. Topsy-like, I suspect "they growed."[1]

The subject I now have to deal with is my engagement. I had grown to like Arthur Ravener very much. I thought we had a great deal in

---

1   In Harriet Beecher Stowe's *Uncle Tom's Cabin* (1852), the uncivilized slave-girl Topsy declares: "I s'pect I just growed. Don't think nobody never made me."

common. I never felt that a woman was a silly chattering doll when I was with him. He would talk upon any subject with me, and never once in all our intercourse did he pay me a single compliment. He never showed that he admired me. All he ever said was that he liked talking to a sensible girl who looked upon the world very much as he did himself.

One evening as I was sitting alone at a detestable "musicale and dance," and wondering as usual why girls wasted their best years in training themselves to shine at such entertainments, I noticed Arthur Ravener and Captain Dillington enter the room. The former looked anxiously around—for me, of course, I knew that; the latter remained standing at the door, where he could see all that was going on. The reception accorded Damon and Pythias was always polite, but never cordial. The men seemed to avoid Captain Dillington, and he usually tacked himself to the skirts of some plump old matron, who talked of nothing more exciting than servants and other domestic relaxations. I imagine that Arthur Ravener must have pursued a similar course before he met me— but then my imagination always did go a long way.

"How do you do, Miss Bouverie?" Arthur Ravener in evening dress was extremely comely, but I could have found it in my heart to wish that he were not so pretty.

"I am so glad you have come, Mr. Ravener, to raise me from the Slough of Despond.[1] I was going gradually down—down—down."

He smiled. I wondered if the little curl in his moustache were natural, or, if not, how he managed to bring it to such perfection. He did not seem to be in a talkative humor, so I felt called upon to make a little conversation. I looked around the room. Of course I knew I could say it was very warm. That is always a safe remark of an evening. It would also not have been out of the way to suggest that there were a great many present.

Ah, there was a good subject for conversation in the young couple opposite, a bride and bridegroom, a couple three months old— matrimonially old, I mean. They were evidently very much enamored and they sickened me. It was very rude of me to take them all in; but they had no idea I was staring at them, so it was all right. I saw him

---

1   The allegorical swamp of despair in John Bunyan's *The Pilgrim's Progress* (1678), into which the hero Christian sinks under the weight of his sins.

take up her dance programme, and scan the names with a frown, she all the time glancing at him with pride and admiration. Then he whispered something in her ear, taking care to brush it with his moustache, and she put one dainty gloved finger on his lip. He sat down beside her and for five minutes they talked so earnestly that I am quite convinced they forgot the fact that they were "in society." I am ashamed to say I listened to them. It was not an edifying conversation. He declared that an evening spent away from her was a terrible ordeal. She asserted that it was a good thing to dance with other men, as the contrast between them and her own dear husband showed her how immeasurably superior he was.

And all this time I forgot I was to amuse my companion. I looked at him. He was listening to the bride and bridegroom also. Shame upon us both.

"Does that interest you?" he asked.

"It disgusts me," I answered emphatically.

"Ah!"—I fancied he had awaited my answer a little anxiously. He looked satisfied.

"I do not believe in such demonstrative devotion," I went on. "There is nothing beautiful in it to me."

"No," he said. "It will never last. In two years it will take a very great effort on her part to keep him at her side. She will by that time probably think the effort not worth making."

I was silent. Perhaps at that moment something told me that my ideas were morbid. It is possible that quick as a flash of lightning my womanhood asserted itself. I say it is possible, and that is all.

"Elsie."

It was the first time he had uttered my Christian name. There was nothing at all tender in the way he pronounced it. I blushed slightly and looked a little conscious. Of course I could make no answer, I sat silent and eyed my gloves (which were rather soiled, by the bye, and not worth eyeing).

"Elsie," he said, "you criticise the conversation of that young couple opposite. But put yourself in her place. Would you prefer your husband to sit calmly by your side, and talk,—perhaps as you and I have talked so often,—quietly, undemonstratively, and sensibly? Would you be satisfied to marry a man who absolutely declined to be the conventional lover, writing ballads to your eyebrows,[1] and extolling your virtues, real and imaginary, while the love fever lasted?"

His face was very pale, and his hands nervously clutched the side of my chair, as he leaned slightly towards me.

"Yes, I would be satisfied," I said.

At that moment I felt acutely happy. Of course I knew to what he was coming. I always laugh when I read novels in which the heroines "look up with large surprised eyes," or "innocently wonder" what a proposing lover means. A girl always knows when a man is asking her to marry him. If he expressed himself in Chinese or Hindostanee she would understand him just as well.

I felt I could be happy with Arthur Ravener. He was entirely different to any other man I had met, and the difference seemed to me, then, to be in his favor.

"Elsie," he said, in very agitated tones, "you have remarked very often that you despised these demonstrative beings. When we first met, you told me frequently that I was different—that you found pleasure in my company. I have seen your face brighten when I approached, and, Elsie, I am emboldened by these signs of your esteem, to ask you to be my wife."

I put my hand quietly in his. You, readers, who have perhaps disapproved of my flippancy, will be astonished to hear that for the moment it left me completely. I was deeply moved by Arthur Ravener's proposal. I was delighted. I really believe I felt as an engaged girl ought to feel,—full of admiration for the man who had honored her, and keenly alive to the fact that this world was after all a good place in which to be.

I looked at Arthur. His face was livid. Its startling pallor gave me a shock. I forgot everything for the moment in my anxiety for his present welfare.

"You are ill?" I said.

He looked at me in surprise.

"No," he replied in a low tone. "I am well. Should I not be well"— with a great effort and a strained smile—"when you have just accepted my—my suit?"

---

1   "And then the lover, / Sighing like a furnace, with a woeful ballad / Made to his mistress' eyebrow." *As You Like It* (II.vii.146-48).

Have you ever experienced the unpleasant sensation of knowing that somebody was staring at you, and been impelled to look in their direction? Of course you have. So you will not be surprised if I tell you that I turned from Arthur Ravener and glanced toward the door. Captain Dillington had been staring at me. He looked confused, I am glad to say, when I returned his stare with interest. In fact he turned immediately away, and began an animated conversation with one of his favorite plump matrons.

"Arthur," I said, impulsively, "I know you and Captain Dillington are such great friends that I want to ask you if he likes me?"

There was no coquetry veiled in this question. I sincerely wished to know how I stood (to use a commercial expression) with the bosom friend of my affianced husband.

Arthur Ravener positively started at my question. For a few seconds he seemed unable to answer.

"I—I am sure he does," he stammered at last. "Yes, Elsie, Captain Dillington does like you. I— I am sure of it. Set your mind at rest."

"Pooh!" said I, inelegantly, feeling that Richard was himself again.[1] "My mind is quite at rest. I'm not going to marry you both, you know"—a remark that was neither pretty nor funny, but vulgar. My carriage had been announced and Arthur was fastening my "*sortie de bal*"[2] around me. In the hall stood Captain Dillington. He bowed and then extended his hand to me.

"May I congratulate you, Miss Bouverie?" he asked.

"You may," I answered blushingly. Then it occurred to me that it was rather strange Captain Dillington should know anything about my engagement. Arthur had not left my side since I had accepted him as my future husband. Then I reflected that Arthur and the Captain were great friends; that the Captain probably knew that Arthur intended asking me to be his wife; that he had seen us in earnest conversation, noticed my "happy expression," and put two and two together—an arithmetical process practiced by many. Still, I was not quite satisfied, although I decided that it would be better to appear so.

"I trust we shall see a great deal of each other"—after a pause—"later."

He had made this identical speech the other day, I remembered.

---

1   "Richard was himself again" is a line from playwright Colley Cibber's hapless 1699 adaptation of Shakespeare's *Richard III* (1591).

2   Cloak worn over an evening gown.

"I hope so," said I. I would try and like him for Arthur's sake, though I was perfectly convinced I should not succeed. The hall door was open. Arthur came down the steps with me. He was still pale.

"Good-night, Arthur," I said, extending my hand.

"Good-night."

His fingers scarcely closed around mine. I had shaken hands with him a dozen times during our acquaintance, and had always told him he ought to take lessons in the art. But his salutation had never been so coldly inexpressive as to-night it seemed to me. I shivered slightly, then drew myself into the obscurity of the carriage and rolled home.

Chapter 7

ARTHUR was very anxious that our engagement should be a short one. My mother would have been perfectly satisfied to have escorted me to the altar on the day following our betrothal, if fashion had established any precedent for such a course. But no, she could not remember any respectable folks marrying after an engagement of less than three months.

"People might talk," she said, and I knew that settled it. There was no more awful possibility. An earthquake would have been pleasant, and a conflagration merely an episode in comparison.

"I don't see why Arthur is in such a hurry," she went on. "Really, you have given him no cause for jealousy; your conduct is always irreproachable. In fact if I were a man I should run a mile to avoid you. I have often thought that your manners must be far from attractive to the other sex."

"Thanks, mother."

"I am sure I am very pleased that it is all going to end so happily, but I cannot consent to your marriage in less than three months. No such case can I remember, except, of course, that of Lady Stitzleton's daughter, which is too shocking for me to discuss with you. Tell Arthur he must wait for three months. I can't for the life of me understand his hurry. You will excuse me for saying it, Elsie, but I confess he does not seem to be particularly—"

"Tender, do you mean, mother?"

"*Épris*[1] is an excellent word to use in this case," said my parent. "If you cannot understand it, however, you can substitute tender. Of course I know that it is very bad form to make any demonstrations in society, but when alone, a little effusiveness is entirely pardonable. You and Arthur were in the library together for a few minutes the other night—perfectly proper of course. As I happened to pass the room, I looked in, prompted of course by my motherly interest. You were at one end of the room, he at the other, and I—"

"Never mind," I said hastily, reddening with vexation. "It shall be as you say—three months."

I stalked from the room thoroughly annoyed. I did not dare to ask myself the cause of my ill temper. Demonstrations of affection I had frequently declared disgusted me, and I had engaged myself to a man who confessed that he thought as I did. I had no reason to complain of Arthur. His behavior toward me had not changed in the slightest since our engagement. He had not attempted to avail himself of the privileges which books on etiquette (I had glanced through them) accord to engaged couples. He had never kissed me, nor hinted at the slightest inclination to do so.

I loved Arthur Ravener, I was proud of the prospect of becoming his wife; but—lest my future history be considered inconsistent with that which I have already related—I will frankly admit, at the risk of being called a contemptible humbug, that I should not have objected in the least if Arthur had been just a trifle less glacial. I admit that now; I made no such admission at the time. I only felt a little discontented, and mentally changed the subject when there was any probability of my discovering the reason of my dissatisfaction.

The news of our engagement soon spread. Shall I be considered egotistical if I say that the men who had previously—so it seemed to me—looked down upon Arthur Ravener, now appeared anxious to know him, and apologetically anxious, too? They had evidently more respect for Elsie Bouverie's affianced husband, than for Captain Dillington's bosom friend. It was rather inexplicable to me, but I was pleased nevertheless.

Arthur was a constant visitor at our house. He never brought Captain Dillington with him. Indeed he always seemed to be so embarrassed

---

1   In love; taken with.

when I asked him to do so, that I at last desisted. It was no desire to know the Captain better that prompted me to invite him to join us. He repelled me as no one either before or since has done. But I knew he was my future husband's boon companion, so was perfectly willing to sink my prejudices. I also thought as there was nobody but a blind old bat of a housekeeper in the flat which they had furnished, and in which they lived, that Captain Dillington must feel rather lonely when Arthur was away. Arthur was a very thoughtful young man. He never stayed very late at our house. Although he did not say so, I was convinced that he did not care to leave his friend alone too long. Such consideration for another pleased me. Had I not every right to reason, by analogy, that when I was his wife, he would show me the same devotion?

I thoroughly dreaded the day when I had to tell Letty Bishop of my engagement. I felt that she would be a wet blanket of the most distressing type, and—somehow or other—I wanted to steer as clear of wet blankets as possible. I was agreeably surprised to find that Letty gave my "news" very little attention, for the simple reason that she had similar information to impart. Yes, Letty was engaged. I had known her betrothed for some time, and had included him in the ranks of the men I despised. He was a butterfly. He admired every girl he met, or seemed to do so. However, if Letty was satisfied with him, why, so was I. I was glad to listen to all she had to say about him, as by doing so, I gave her no opportunity to make unpleasant remarks concerning Arthur Ravener. She hoped I would be happy, and laughingly begged me not to hold her responsible for the match. She talked a great deal of nonsense about her Reginald, and I could not get interested. They were evidently a conventionally gushing couple.

"Arthur," said I, that night, adopting my favorite would-be jaunty air, "what will become of Captain Dillington while we are on our honeymoon; there are such a number of places I want to visit, and I'm not going to be hurried." Arthur reddened painfully, and then averted his face. "I was thinking, Elsie," he said with a sickly smile, "that we would abolish that old-fashioned notion of honeymooning, and go immediately after the wedding to your house in Kew."

My mother had presented me with a delightful little villa near Kew Gardens, and it was settled that we were to live there during the first year of our wedded life at any rate. But I could not believe that we were to domesticate ourselves on our wedding day.

"You are joking, Arthur," I said weakly.

"I don't see why," shuffling uneasily on his chair. "I think traveling is an abomination, and, really, you know, honeymoons are not fashionable. Are you—are you" (very anxiously) "very desirous of going out of town?"

"I don't care particularly," I said with magnanimity. "I took it for granted that we should make a trip. I would have preferred it; but, of course, if you would sooner not—"

"What is that, Elsie?"

Enter my maternal parent at an inopportune moment, as usual. She saw we were engaged in discussion and I felt she was anxious to assist us.

"Arthur does not want to take a wedding trip, mother," I said, "and I was telling him that I had been reckoning upon one."

"It is out of fashion, Mrs. Bouverie," remarked Mr. Ravener, looking with appealing eyes at the arbitrator. "I am sure you will agree with me that it is. No one is better acquainted with the usages of society than you are" (deferentially).

Oh, the hypocrite! I knew she would succumb to that, and so did he. If it had not been for that disgustingly polite speech, I felt that she would have decided in favor of the trip, as she had already confided to my care a list of commissions which I was to execute for her in Paris.

"You are right, Arthur," she said, promptly. "Honeymoons are becoming obsolete in the best society. There is something extremely *bourgeois* about them to my mind." There was not the faintest remembrance of the commissions in her tone. Her foible had been touched. Arthur was triumphant, but he looked rather doubtfully at me. He evidently did not want me to think that he was positively averse to a honeymoon.

"Where do you propose going after the wedding?" asked mamma.

"To Tavistock Villa, Kew," was his rejoinder.

"Of course you will not receive for several months?"

"Oh, no—no—," impatiently, "we shall remain in retirement, and see none but—but the immediate family, and—and intimate friends."

Well, I must let Arthur settle such matters, I thought. After all, perhaps he was right. Honeymoons must have distinctly unpleasant features. Traveling was a nuisance, and with the best of intentions, and the largest purse, it was impossible to obtain home comforts at continental hotels, I had heard. When I told Letty Bishop that we had decided to abolish the honeymoon, she opened her eyes in surprise. Was such a thing possible? Surely Arthur Ravener was even more eccentric than she had originally supposed, and she had given him credit for a considerable portion of eccentricity. What! Settle down to common-place matrimony, and receive the butcher, the baker and the greengrocer in the first week of married life! What could he mean?

"Don't be absurd, Letty" I said fretfully, in reply to this outburst. "It was my idea and not his." (There was a whopper, but I felt I must do something desperate.) "I dislike traveling, and I am convinced that we should quarrel before we reached Paris. And then, my dear," faintly "I should not care for my husband to see me—seasick." (That was an inspiration.)

"Well, Elsie, I suppose you know best what you like. It looks queer, though. Honeymoons may not be fashionable in the very, very highest society; but, my dear, you don't belong to the very, very highest society."

"Don't dare to say that to my mother," I cried, "or she would kill you in her frenzied indignation."

I tried to believe that I was satisfied, but I was not. With all my superiority, I was disappointed.

CHAPTER 8

M Y marriage was not a particularly interesting event from an anecdotal standpoint. My mother was far too precisely conventional to allow anything to interfere in the slightest with the rule laid down by that terrible tyrant in petticoats, Mrs. Grundy.[1]

I was rather surprised that Arthur cared for the amount of publicity which I saw would attend the event, but he positively gloried in it. He seemed anxious to have his marriage recorded in the four corners of the globe. The feminine newspaper correspondents, who called to ask for the particulars of Miss Bouverie's bridal dress, Miss Bouverie's trousseau, and Miss Bouverie herself, I had strict injunctions from my betrothed to satisfy as far as possible.

My wedding morning was one in which novelists delight—plenty of sun, and a delightfully invigorating atmosphere. I was as happy as a bird. The prospect of freedom from the hateful society chains, which I felt would in a few years deprive me of my much prized liberty, added to the love which I felt for Arthur Ravener, were the causes of my bliss.

---

1   Character in Thomas Morton's play *Speed the Plough* (1798) and a byword for narrow-mindedness and conventionality.

I was a dainty little bride in my white robes, but I still had the horrible feeling that I was not nearly as pretty as Arthur. The flush on his cheek, his full red lips, long eyelashes, and splendid complexion far surpassed my efforts in those directions. He was more noticed in the church than I was—by which you will perceive that my excitement did not prevent my powers of observation from having full play. Perhaps it was his beauty after all that gained for him the contempt of men. The sterner sex have their weaknesses, and we do not monopolize,—as they are so fond of asserting,—all the petty envy and spite in this world.

I saw all my old friends in the church. My "belongings" certainly out-numbered Arthur's. Two hideous old maiden aunts, one dilapidated uncle, and three lachrymose cousins constituted his force of relatives. I feel it is awful of me to allude in such terms to people who could now claim relationship with myself, but I do not intend to conceal anything from my readers.

A drowsy old minister, so well known that I suppose he thought that any exertion on his part was unnecessary, made us man and wife, and kept his gaze rivetted all the time on the bridesmaids, who imagined they were not paying proper attention on that account, and seemed at a loss to know what to do to get rid of his eyes.

How I should have enjoyed the wedding if it had been somebody else's. Letty and I, in a corner of the church, could have picked everybody to pieces and amused ourselves generally. I can even imagine what I should have said about myself, and I know I should have sworn that Arthur was rouged. My bridesmaids I should have revelled in criticising, because I thoroughly disliked every one of them. My mother had selected them, and I had nothing to do in the matter but submit.

Arthur seemed to be in a dream, from which he only awoke when the reverend gentleman put those extremely leading questions to him. His voice was hoarse as he answered. His hand trembled as he placed the wedding ring on my finger. His fingers were icily cold. Only once did he look at me. I fancied then that there was just a faint tinge of compassion in the glance. I met it with a proud smile. Ah! he little knew what a lucky girl I thought myself.

After the ceremony came a reception and breakfast, at which everybody I had ever seen seemed to be present. In the evening there was to be a ball, at which, of course, we were not to be present. I was glad for once to follow fashion's dictates. Early in the afternoon Arthur and I said good-bye to a few hundred people, and stepping into the carriage which was waiting for us, set out for Tavistock Villa.

* * * * *

As we rolled away from the metropolis towards our country home, I tried hard to direct my thoughts into those channels through which I felt they ought to flow. Here was I, a bride of a few hours, leaving home without a regret and without a reflection of "childhood's associations," the new life, and other pathetic subjects over which nineteenth-century brides are popularly supposed to become sentimental. I must put it all down to the flippancy of my nature.

Arthur made no attempt to break the silence. If I was an unusual bride, certainly he was the most utterly unconventional bridegroom it was possible to imagine. His eyes were fixed dreamily upon two little fleecy clouds which were floating about artlessly above us. He could not have looked more hopelessly subdued if he had been sitting in a funeral coach, and going to bury a friend. I suppose my glance aroused him.

"Are you enjoying this ride, Elsie?" he asked, kindly.

"Yes," I answered, noting his effort to amuse me, and feeling grateful to him for it. "I suppose," I said, laughing, "that all these people would be staring at us if they knew we were bride and bridegroom. They take us for brother and sister, undoubtedly."

"Or an old married couple," he added, smiling.

"I wonder if we ever shall be old commonplace people," I went on happily. "Imagine us fifty years from now, Arthur—you a nice reminiscent old man with white hair (you see I decline to think of you as cross and crotchety), sitting on one side of the fire, and I, a talkative old body, having outlived every weakness but that furnished by the tongue, which no woman could outlive if she were a female Methuselah."[1]

---

1   969-year-old Biblical patriarch.

Arthur laughed, and seemed for the first time since I had known him to be perfectly at his ease. I put my hand ("my little gloved hand," as my friends the novelists would say) on his arm. He might have squeezed it if he had chosen. I am quite sure I should not have objected, except perhaps by a little maidenly coyness, which does not amount to very much. Arthur, however, took no notice whatever of my innocent little hand. Indeed, by a movement he made as if to look out of the carriage window, he contrived to shake it off. This I did not notice at the time, but as I have since become accustomed to think and brood over every little incident of those days, I have remembered it.

After that we talked merrily for the remainder of the ride. I was determined that I would start my married life with mirth. Men hate miserable, doleful women. Nine out of ten of them would sooner have an ugly wife who laughed than a pretty one who cried. Now I resolved that Arthur Ravener should have a wife who was both pretty and jolly. So I was as lively as I could be.

Tavistock Villa came into sight all too soon. It was a pretty red brick house, which I shall not attempt to describe. I am an utter failure from an architectural standpoint, and only know two things in that line: that some houses are Gothic and some are not. The house had been the gift of my mother, and it had been furnished by my husband. We went in.

I was loud in my admiration of his taste as soon as we had passed the front door. Every article of furniture seemed to have been selected with excellent judgment. I will not weary my readers with a description of tables and chairs and carpets, which have nothing to do with my story.

"Here are your rooms, Elsie," said Arthur, opening the door of an exquisite little boudoir, "and you can be as completely alone here as though you were Robinson Crusoe on the desert island."

"I shall not want to be alone very often, dear," I said, gushingly.

"I have a couple of rooms on the other side of the house fitted up for myself, to smoke and write in," he went on, rather hesitatingly, paying no attention to my pretty little speech. "You see I do a little literary work, and I—I—do not want to be disturbed."

"You shall not be disturbed, Arthur," I said, dutifully. "Let me go and inspect your rooms, please."

He looked annoyed. "They are in great disorder, Elsie," he said, "and I don't think you had better venture into them."

"I feel a wifely interest in them, dear," I pleaded with a smile.

"Not now," he said hastily.

"I believe you're a Bluebeard, Arthur, and that the bodies of a dozen preceding Mrs. Ravener's lie festering in that room. I shall wait until you go out, like the last and surviving Mrs. Bluebeard did, and then make a voyage of exploration."

"You will not be repaid for your trouble," he said, smiling. But he was vexed. I could see it.

"I don't see why your rooms are at one side of the house and mine at the other, Arthur," I said. "It's very unsociable, I am sure."

"Nonsense," was my husband's testy response. "Every man ought to have a den of his own, in which he can smoke, or read, or write."

"I know it," was my prompt rejoinder, "but, though it is an odious thing to say, I could have permitted you to smoke in my boudoir."

"You are not your mother's daughter," he said, laughing rather uneasily.

Arthur then introduced me to a young French girl, whom he had engaged as my maid. Marie was certainly a pretty woman, not a bit Gallic to look at. She had honest gray eyes, an excellent complexion, and brown hair. I liked her appearance and thanked Arthur for his thoughtfulness. Since I had entered Tavistock Villa I had seen nothing but evidences of his earnest desire to make my life there pleasant. When we had finished inspecting our new home, or rather, when I had come to the end of my gushing superlatives, and his services as guide were no longer required, we decided to take a stroll through the pretty Kew roads, and return in time for dinner. He led the way and I followed. Down the dusty, charming little lanes we went, talking all the time, and laughing frequently. I had never known Arthur so entertaining as he was that afternoon. He told me stories of his school days, of his dead father and mother, of his musical studies, and of all his old friends. I was not obliged to catechize him. He talked freely and seemed to enjoy it.

That was a delightful afternoon. I shall always remember it. I can see the delicious little town as I saw it before it became hateful to me. I can recollect my first impressions of the sunny thoroughfares, the lovely gardens, and the comfortable, unpretentious houses.

It was dark when we turned back. I was rather tired. The day had been somewhat fatiguing. It is rather an unusual event in one's life to be married. Arthur might have offered me his arm, I thought. But he made no attempt to do so, as I walked by his side. We found dinner awaiting us. It was a very elaborate meal, with I don't know how many courses. I seemed to have come to the end of my good spirits. I did not feel inclined to talk, and as Arthur appeared to be wrapped in his own thoughts (not agreeable ones, either, if I can judge from his face) silence prevailed. It seemed strange to be sitting there at dinner with him. I felt rather sorry that he had objected to the honeymoon; I really began to wonder, now that I had seen Kew, how we could possibly amuse ourselves there for any length of time. I wondered more for his sake than for my own, as I know that to men variety is always charming.

"Elsie," said Arthur, breaking the silence at last, "do you think, dear, that you could get along without me this evening. You have Marie—and—and I must run up to town?"

My husband was very intently regarding the walnuts on his plate as he asked this question—very intently indeed.

"Of course, Arthur," I replied, quickly, "if you must leave me, go by all means. I would not like to interfere with any of your business arrangements, or—"

"You are a good little woman," he said, but he did not look into my face and thank me for what I really considered a sacrifice. I thought it was rather strange that he should be obliged to go up to London so soon. Surely he could have transacted any business he might have had before we started, though as Arthur was "a gentleman" (in the language of the directory) I was at a loss to imagine what business could call him away, and surely the poorest commercial drudge took a holiday and devoted the first week at least of his married life, exclusively to his wife. However, there might be a hundred reasons for his departure, and I had no doubt that when I had earned the right to know what they were, he would permit me to do so.

"I may be rather late, Elsie," he said hastily, "but do not worry." He left the room a few moments later, and returned overcoated and ready to start.

"Amuse yourself, Elsie," he said. "Do anything you like, and try not to be homesick. Good-bye, dear."

He was leaving without kissing me. Though I had protested so often that I would not tolerate a demonstrative husband, Arthur's conduct seemed so strange, that a feeling of resentment came over me. I did not look up.

"Good-bye, Elsie," repeated my husband, uneasily approaching me. "What is the matter?"

"Nothing."

"Well, good-bye."

"Good-bye."

He started for the door, and the next instant I was after him. "Arthur," I cried impulsively, "you shall not go from me in that way, even if you intend being away only half-an-hour. Kiss me."

He bent forward and touched my lips with his, so coldly and undemonstratively, that I shrank back, and looked at him in surprise. I felt chilled. "Come back early," I said, returning to the room hastily, anxious to be away from him. I decided that I would go to my boudoir, so calling Marie to keep me company, we went upstairs to that cosy little apartment.

I had a long evening before me and the prospect was not a lively one. I could not feel at home in Tavistock Villa, which a few hours ago I had never even seen. It seemed to me that Arthur ought to have stayed with me, no matter what sacrifice he made. I knew very little about brides and bridegrooms beyond what I had read in novels, nine-tenths of which either ended with a couples' engagement, or began, in early married life.

I went to the drawing-room and tried the piano, but somehow I could derive no amusement from it. I glanced at a couple of books, but their unreality disgusted me. The heroine in one of them was sentimental to idiocy, with a flower-like face and violet eyes, while the principal character in the other was a hoyden with whom I could find no sympathy. I went back to my boudoir. It was delightfully comfortable. I installed myself in an easy-chair, made Marie sit opposite, poor girl, and then closed my eyes.

"Is it that Madame is recently married?" asked Marie presently, more, I felt convinced, to break a silence that was becoming oppressive than from any real interest in me or my belongings.

"Did you not know that we were married this morning, Marie?" I demanded rather sharply.

"*Comment!*"[1] She was interested now to such an extent that the exclamation she uttered was in her own language. "You were married this morning—to-day?"—with incredulity.

"Certainly," said I. "When my husband engaged you did he not tell you that he was about to be married?"

"No, Madame," replied Marie. "When I called regarding the advertisement he told me I was to be maid to his wife. In consequence I thought you were long married. But, Madame, pardon me, if you were married today, why is it that Monsieur leaves you so soon alone?"

"Why not?" I was furious with her and would have given a sovereign for the privilege of administering a sharp slap. I could not answer her question. I knew of no answer. It was evident, however, from her unfeigned surprise that Arthur had done a very unusual thing when he left me alone on my wedding-day. My instinct told me that he was entirely in the wrong. Marie, however, had confirmed this hardly admitted view. She sat with her mouth slightly open, staring at me in such unpleasant surprise that I was forced to turn my face away.

"You are very rude, Marie," I said at last, desperately angry at the girl's stupidly apparent astonishment. "Don't you know that it is the height of impoliteness to stare at anybody like that? I am surprised at you, a Frenchwoman, behaving in such a manner."

It did me good to manifest a little surprise on my own account. I saw no reason why she should be permitted to monopolize it all.

"Madame will excuse me," said the girl quickly. "I am not yet entirely used to English customs. It seemed so droll to me that a bridegroom should leave his bride—Madame will pardon me."

I rose and paced up and down the room. What a fool I was to worry myself about such trifles. Arthur had shown nothing but the most delicate consideration for me up to the present, and yet because he asked my permission to absent himself for a few hours on our wedding-day, I worked myself up into a state of nervous excitement on the ground that the proceeding happened to be a little unusual. Pshaw! what nonsense. Had we not a whole lifetime to spend together? How could I be so ridiculous? "Ha! Ha! Ha!" I burst out laughing. Poor Marie must have

---

1   What!

experienced another surprise concerning English customs. She looked up, her gray eyes round as saucers.

"Is Madame ill?"

"Fiddlesticks!" I exclaimed, with unpardonable inelegance. "Let us come into the drawing-room, and I will teach you how we waltz over here."

Alas! with all the efforts I made, the time dragged horribly. It was now midnight, and there had been nothing to break the monotony of the evening. I wondered what they were doing at home. Dancing, of course, for my sake. The ball was now at its height, and my mother was in a state of dignified ecstasy. Marie sat in a low armchair, yawning. She tried to yawn gracefully, I am sure; but it was quite impossible.

"Go to bed, Marie," I said, peremptorily, at one o'clock.

"I will wait with Madame," was the reply.

And again we sat down to the contemplation of each other's charms. How lonely it was! We made a round of the house and saw that everything had been properly secured for the night, simply because I felt so nervous that I could not sit there inactive. I will not attempt to describe all the weird noises we heard, because everybody who has sat up in the early hours of the morning knows exactly what they are. At three o'clock I started violently. I think I must have been asleep. The striking of the clock in the hall aroused me.

"Marie," I said a few minutes later, "I am going to bed. My husband will not be back to-night, that is very sure. I will wait no longer. Goodnight."

To my surprise Marie kissed me. I remember hoping that she did not intend to do so every night. I hated affectionate people as I have already said often enough. I was almost dead with fatigue. I went to my room, undressed quickly, and was soon in a deep, dreamless sleep, from which I awoke when my watch told me it was ten o'clock, and the sun was dancing merrily over the daintily carpeted floor.

CHAPTER 9

I FELT thoroughly good-natured, and was determined to be as smilingly gracious as I possibly could when I met my eccentric husband. Of course I should not even allude to his most unaccountable behavior, but I had no doubt at all that he would be utterly repentant, and that his remorse would even go so far as to melt the ice of his manners.

I selected one of the nattiest little morning dresses that my trousseau contained. It was one of those charmingly devised costumes that would render the most hideous woman acceptable. Now, I was not hideous by any means, and when I took a final look at myself before descending, I had never appeared more comely, I thought. In spite of my early morning vigil, the roses bloomed becomingly on my cheeks, and my eyes sparkled with health.

Down the broad staircase I sailed. I was Mrs. Arthur Ravener now, so it would not do to "trip." Matrons sail. That term has a very dignified sound in my ears. Before entering the breakfast-room, I peeped coyly in. Yes, there sat my husband, deep in a newspaper. He had already begun breakfast, and must have poured out his coffee, and buttered his toast with his own manly fingers. I walked in.

"Good-morning, Arthur," I said, coquettishly, taking my seat at the head of the table. Perhaps I had better confess that I felt a little nervous.

"You are late, Elsie," remarked my husband, laying down his paper. "I thought I would take the initiative and begin breakfast. I hope you do not think it impolite on my part?"

"Not a bit, I shall soon catch you up. I'm as hungry as a hunter. This Kew air seems to be invigorating."

In reality I had no appetite at all. The thought of breakfast sickened me, but I was determined, with all the perversity of my sex, that he should not know it.

"I am glad of that, Elsie," said Arthur, smiling at me kindly. He rose, poured me out a cup of coffee, buttered a slice of toast for me, helped me to some cold partridge, and went back to his seat. He had looked just a trifle uneasy, I fancied, when I entered, but he had now completely recovered. The awful idea occurred to me that he would make no comments whatever on his absence last night. As I had always heard that between husband and wife there should be complete confidence, I resolved that I would do violence to my feelings and broach the subject, as a matter of principle, if for no other reason. I did not want abject apologies, but I was not going to be treated with such sublime disrespect.

"Will you have half my newspaper, Elsie?" asked Arthur, as I sat silently devouring my partridge, with all my good temper rapidly vanishing.

"Thank you." He handed me a couple of sheets.

"They have given a splendid account of the wedding," he said, "and I suppose that all England knows about it now."

"Why are you so anxious for all England to be informed that you are a Benedict?"[1] I enquired scornfully.

He reddened and made no reply. I glanced carelessly through the half column of silly gush, learned that I had made a very interesting bride, and noticed some very flattering allusions to my husband. "After the reception," I read aloud, "the bride and bridegroom left for Kew, where they will spend the honeymoon in their handsome home, Tavistock Villa." "They might have added," I said, laying down the paper and trying to speak indifferently, "that the bridegroom returned

---

1   In Shakespeare's comedy *Much Ado About Nothing* (ca. 1599), Benedick, a confirmed bachelor, repeatedly denounces love and marriage, only to confess his love publicly for Beatrice, the woman with whom he constantly squabbles.

to London early in the evening, and was back in Kew again in time for breakfast."

I leaned forward in my chair to enjoy the effect of my sarcasm.

"Don't be foolish, Elsie," said my husband, from behind his newspaper, "I told you I was obliged to go up to London and I know you are too sensible a little woman to stand in my way in a case like that."

"Stand in your way!" My cheeks were the color of peonies. I was horribly indignant.

"Elsie," said Arthur, "I don't want you to be vexed. You are very young, and—and—well, I am older. There was really no cause for you to worry last night. This house is as safe as a—a bank. Kew is a very quiet, respectable sort of place, and such things as burglars are almost unknown. I—I—was going to telegraph you that I was unable to return, but—but—"

"But what?"—sharply.

"I was afraid a telegram might alarm you. Now, Elsie, there is not a soul who knows anything about this—this—this affair, and I would not talk about it."

"Talk about it?" I exclaimed in angry surprise. "With whom?"

"W-with anybody. With your mother, for example."

"Oh, no," I laughed satirically. "It would not interest her. I am not a gossip, Arthur. Our affairs can interest nobody but ourselves."

"You are a thoroughly sensible girl, Elsie," said Arthur, with what sounded like a little sigh of relief. "Now, hurry with your breakfast, dear, and I'll take you for a nice long drive, and we'll have luncheon out."

That restored my drooping spirits more than anything else could have done. I forgot all about my grievances. After all they were not very formidable. If I never had anything more to contend with during my life, I might think myself fortunate.

It was a glorious day and I was determined to enjoy myself. Arthur had a neat little phaeton waiting at the door, and into it we stepped. Arthur took the whip, and off we went at a delightful rate. How keenly invigorating the air was! I thought of Letty Bishop and remembered how she hated such drives. The bane of her life was a red nose, and she would have had an extremely conspicuous one had she been with us today. After a delicious drive of a couple of hours, we "put up" at a little hotel, and Arthur ordered a most tempting luncheon. What a blessing an appetite is! We were both hungry. The last vestige of my woes vanished as I found myself opposite to a plate of succulent natives.[1] My good spirits must have been contagious. Arthur caught them, and was his own amiable, amusing self. He talked and laughed and told some excellent stories. I had never found myself with so agreeable a companion—and to think that he was my husband! What a senseless girl I had been to worry. I promised myself that for the future I would indulge in no more idiocy.

"Just think, Arthur," I said, as he dallied with some cheese (dallying with cheese is my own idea) and I made a combination of almonds and raisins, "Marie imagined we were old married people. You never told her that we were just married—you sly boy."

"Did you?" It was really very strange why Arthur should get so uncomfortable at my little innocent remarks.

"Of course I did. I don't propose to sail under false colors, as an antiquated dowager."

"What did Marie say?" with eagerness.

"She was very, very surprised. She thought you were so droll to go off to the City as you did. I was angry with her, and she said she was not accustomed to English habits." I spoke cheerfully; I had quite forgiven him.

My husband did not look pleased. "I do wish you would not chatter about me and my business, Elsie," he said with marked vexation. "If Marie makes any more impertinent remarks, send her away."

I said nothing. Arthur was an oddity—*voilà tout*,[2] as my mother loved to remark. I must give way to him in a proper, wifely manner. I was resolved that "amiability, amiability, always amiability," should be my motto. So I cracked him three most inviting filberts and laid them as a peace offering on his plate.

"By-the-bye, Elsie," said my husband presently, as we were thinking about departing, "Captain Dillington is coming to dinner tonight."

If he had given me a sound box on the ears I could not have been more disagreeably surprised. I lost all idea of keeping to the text of my motto. What did he mean by asking this man to our house, the day following our marriage? Why, my mother had told me that as we were

---

1   Oysters.

2   That's all.

not going on a wedding trip, we must live in retirement for a month. I had Fashion on my side, thank goodness.

"To-night!" I exclaimed aghast.

"Why not?"

"It is not usual, Arthur. Why c-can't we have a nice l-little dinner alone?"

"Nonsense. It is perfectly proper to ask one's parents and most intimate friends to the house, I am sure. Elsie, I cannot put Captain Dillington off. You—you do not want me to do so."

He appealed to me. What could I say? I felt that an untruth would be the only thing that would please him. If I told the truth it would be to the effect that I hated Captain Dillington at all times, and my hatred was, if possible, intensified, just now.

"No, no," I said, choking down a little sob, "don't put him off. When d-did you invite him, Arthur?"

"When?"

"Yes, when?"

"Last night."

"Oh, you saw him last night. D-did you meet him accidentally?"

"Elsie!" exclaimed Arthur fretfully, "don't catechize me. What makes you so cross? I want to amuse you. I am doing all I can to prevent you feeling in the least homesick. I am very, very anxious for you to be happy, and you look miserable because I ask my greatest friend to the house. Why you yourself said that our great friendship was a source of admiration to you. It first attracted your attention."

He spoke the truth. I had said all that and more. Of course I meant it. I did admire sincere friendship—but surely there was a limit to all things. His affection for Captain Dillington certainly need not interfere with his love for me. I was his wife after all. I would not argue, however. Captain Dillington was to come to dinner. So be it. I would reserve a careful analysis of my statements for a future occasion.

"I am foolish, Arthur," I said, rising. "Come, let us go home, and see that at any rate Captain Dillington will have something to eat."

He took my hand and pressed it lightly. His eyes looked into mine with gratitude clearly expressed in their depths. Yes, my self-sacrifice had its reward. I jumped at the crumbs he threw to me, and swallowed them ravenously. I could have digested more with perfect facility. We went back to Tavistock Villa. The drive home, however, was not very pleasant. The atmosphere seemed to be less invigorating. There were clouds in the sky. The horses were tired, and the dust, which the wheels of the phaeton sent up in columns, almost blinded me.

There were but few arrangements to make for the accommodation of our guest. I made myself charming in a dress of pale blue silk, and went down to the drawing-room. Captain Dillington was already there. He and Arthur stood with their backs to the door as I appeared. They were in earnest conversation, and did not even hear me enter.

"Good evening, Captain Dillington," I said affably, extending my hand.

"Ah, Mrs. Ravener—delighted I am sure." There was horrible unction in his greeting. Was I so blinded by prejudice that everything this man did simply nauseated my soul?

"I do sincerely hope that I am not intruding," he went on blandly. "I told Arthur—"

"Not at all," I said in the tones which a refrigerator would use if it could speak. "How are things in London?"

"You were there but yesterday," with a smile, as though he were determined that I should not forget this. "There is positively nothing new—positively nothing."

The announcement of dinner was a welcome sound in my ears. How heartily I wished before commencing it that it was over. It was not a very trying ordeal, however. My husband and Captain Dillington talked on a variety of subjects, and I did not feel it at all necessary, under the circumstances, to include myself in the conversation. I did not absolutely wish Captain Dillington to feel that his presence was unpleasant, but I likewise did not wish him to congratulate himself on the fact that it was pleasant.

After dinner I rose, and, leaving them to their own resources, went into the drawing-room. I played some of my beautiful "*morceaux de salon*," not because I liked them, but because it passed away the time and made a noise. I was not happy enough to indulge in any of the dainty little pieces in which I generally delighted when alone.

It was ten o'clock before they joined me. Captain Dillington congratulated me upon my "exquisite touch" and said a few conventional things, after which the two men sat down to a game of chess.

What a wearisome parody of amusement chess is, in my opinion; I suppose I am not intellectual enough to appreciate it. I remember I once tried to learn it, but I never could remember how to move the pawns, and always called out "check" at the most ridiculously inopportune moments.

I sat in a low rocking chair and yawned desperately. I made no pretense of occupying myself with fancy work, which I despised most cordially.

I took up the *Times* and tried to get interested in the agony column.[1] I wondered what it was that A. B. would hear of to his advantage if he communicated with Mr. Snipper of Lincoln's Inn Fields. I tried to imagine what a weight of woe would be lifted from the heart of Lottie L. when she read that all would be forgiven if she would only return to Jack D.

"You are tired, Elsie," said Arthur at last, pausing in an interesting move as I yawned in an ultra-outrageous manner.

"Very," I said.

Then he forgot that I was there.

At midnight they were still hard at it. My eyelids were closing with fatigue. I was raging inwardly (which ought to have kept me awake, but it did not).

At one o'clock I could stand it no longer. I rose from my chair and went towards the door.

"Good-night," I said, looking straight in front of me. If they replied, I did not hear them. I fled to my room.

---

1   Advice column.

CHAPTER 10

I COULD not sleep. I tried my hardest to woo the old humbug Morpheus,[1] who is always on hand when not wanted, but fails to respond to urgent appeals. I was as wide awake as I had been in the early morning, with the sole difference that I was now feverish and oppressed. I rang the bell that communicated with Marie's room. She responded to the call, looking horribly sleepy and unlovely, poor girl.

"Marie," I said, "I cannot sleep. Would you mind sitting with me until morning? I don't know what is the matter with me, but I am too wide awake even to doze."

I threw open the window of my room and let the cool night breezes blow through my refractory tresses. It was a glorious moonlight night, and as I looked at the pretty little gardens in the lovely blue-white illumination, I felt less ill at ease.

"Madame will take cold," Marie ventured to remark.

"Madame is not so fragile as she looks," was my reply. A crunching sound below made me start and look down. Surely I could not be mistaken. My husband and Captain Dillington were in the garden, slowly

---

1   Greek god of dreams.

walking up and down, arm-in-arm. They were smoking placidly, and conversing in low, earnest tones, between puffs. I sent Marie to bed with a promptitude which must have caused her considerable astonishment. Truly by this time her ideas of English customs must have been of the Munchausen order.[1] I did not know Arthur was so fond of nocturnal rambles. How glad I should have been had he asked me to join him. Perhaps he supposed that I was a delicate little reared-in-the-lap-of-luxury maiden and felt that my wifely duties consisted in looking pretty and sitting at the head of the dinner-table. What a mistake he made!

I could see the two men distinctly, though they could not detect me behind the pretty plants that adorned my windows. I could hear them talking, though it was impossible to distinguish what they said while they were at a distance. They were approaching me, however, and as they came nearer their words fell distinctly on my ears. "She is a dear little thing, Dill," said Arthur nervously.

"What of that?" came quickly from the lips of the Captain.

"She deserves a better husband. I am beginning—"

"Don't begin then," angrily, "your wife is a mere child. Give her a comfortable home, handsome dresses, and the thousand little comforts that women love, and she will be your devoted admirer for many years to come. Don't let her read trashy books, and when you go into society, monopolize her yourself."

"Perhaps you are right, Dill," sighed Arthur, "you always are, old man, but—poor Elsie!"

I could hear no more. They were already far away, and I had strained my ears—if that be possible—to understand this much of their conversation. I am not sentimental, as I think I have already proved. It may have been the strange influences of the hour that unnerved me. The tears coursed slowly down my cheeks. The garden was blotted from my sight.

The conversation between my husband and Captain Dillington had been couched in the language to which I had been accustomed all my life, and yet I could not have understood its meaning less, if it had been spoken in Greek. Why did I deserve a better husband? Arthur was as

---

1   Baron Karl Friedrich von Münchhausen (1720-1797), German aristocrat who was famous for his outlandish tales of adventure.

good as I was, I loyally believed. He might have a few eccentricities, but I had more faults. For each of his eccentricities I had two faults. I was flippant, childish, emotional. Perhaps, too, I myself was eccentric. Letty Bishop had always said so; my mother had ever declared it. It was Arthur who merited a better wife, not I who deserved a better husband. He had been rather inattentive to me during these early days of our married life. The only reason could be that I was not sufficiently attractive to him. I had not yet studied him enough to conform to his views. It surely was a wife's duty to conform to her husband's views, and not a husband's obligation to regulate himself to his wife's ideas. You see what a dutiful little lady I was inclined to be.

I kept my eyes fixed upon the garden, and longed for an opportunity to go to Arthur and settle any little difficulties before they widened into an impassable gulf.

The opportunity came. With joy I saw Captain Dillington leave Arthur, throw aside his cigarette, and go into the house. I presumed that he intended to continue as our guest. I had made no preparation for him, however.

I dressed quicker than I had ever done before in my life, and throwing a long cloak over me, rushed down the stairs, pell mell, forgetting my previous views upon the matronly "sail." It was very dark in the hall. The lights had been diminished to a glimmer. I stumbled on my way to the door, and should have fallen if some one had not come to my aid.

"Mrs. Ravener!" exclaimed Captain Dillington—for he it was—in great surprise, "what are you doing about at this hour?"

"Have I not as much right to be about, as you call it, as you and my husband?"

He made no answer. I could not see his face. "You were not going out, surely, Mrs. Ravener?" he asked, a few seconds later.

"I was going out, and I am going out," said I with beautiful redundancy.

"You will take cold," he suggested, quickly; "the night air is very chilly, you know."

"Good-night, Captain Dillington,"—preparing to join Arthur. "I presume you intend remaining with us. You do not think of going up to town at this hour?" Sweetly hospitable, but I could not help it.

"Oh, no."

"*Au revoir*, then."

"Let me take you to your husband, Mrs. Ravener; you may stumble again, you know."

"Thank you, Captain Dillington, I can find my way."

"Let me accompany you; I am in no hurry to retire."

"No," I said sharply. "I should make no more ceremony with you than you do with me, if I wanted you. I wish to see Arthur, alone—alone, Captain Dillington."

"As you wish." He shrugged his shoulders, and with his unctuous smile, left me. I went forthwith into the gardens.

Arthur had taken possession of a rustic seat. His delicate profile was clearly defined in the moonlight. He was evidently deep in thought—and I suppose he had no idea that his reflections were about to be interrupted. I walked quickly across the damp, dewy grass, and before he knew it, I was seated beside him.

"Arthur."

He started violently, and almost jumped from his seat.

"Elsie!" he exclaimed. "You here, and at this time. Why did you come? You will take a severe cold. You should not have ventured out."

"Would you mind very much if I did take a severe cold?"

"How can you be so foolish, Elsie?" he asked testily. "Of course, I should mind. Have I not charge of your future life? What is putting such strange ideas into your head, dear?"

"Arthur," I said slowly, "I was at my open window just now, and I heard you talking with Captain Dillington. Oh, I did not distinguish much of what you said," I went on, as I noticed he looked disconcerted. "You declared that I deserved a better husband, and Captain Dillington thought that I was a mere child, and that as long as I had a comfortable home, I should be happy. Am I a mere child, Arthur?"

"Are you?" he asked slowly, not meeting my eyes. "If you are, Elsie—and I believe it now, as I believed it when I first met you—try and remain so. Elsie, dear, be innocent and good as you now are as long as you can, for your own sake, and—" there were tears in his eyes—"for mine. If you only knew, dear, how anxious I am that your life should be a happy one—that through no fault of mine you should suffer—" he was agitated as I had never seen any man before. "Why did you come out to me here, Elsie. Why—why did you come?" this in feverish, excited tones.

"Because I love you, Arthur," I exclaimed vehemently, throwing my arms around his neck, all my theories as to the absurdity of demonstrative behavior gone to the winds.

"Don't, Elsie," he said, unclasping my arms.

"I will," I said, "I am your wife; you have no right to repulse me. Arthur," noticing with surprise his look of alarm, "you prefer Captain Dillington's company to mine. You selected him for your midnight stroll. You—you—you think n-n-nothing of me. Oh, Arthur, you are unkind, cruel, heartless."

I burst into a passion of tears, which were as much a surprise to me as they were to Arthur. It must have been years since I had wept, and now I was succumbing to a regular storm. I became hysterical. I remember feeling that I was making a fool of myself, and trying to laugh with the most ridiculous result.

"I may be a child," I sobbed, "but I don't want to be slighted; you—you are slighting me. You—do not care for me. You do not,—no—no—you do not. You hate me, I know it. You—wish—you were n-not married. Let me go home. I—I don't want to go, but—if—y-you think it would be better—Why don't you speak? Speak, Arthur, speak."

By this time I was beside myself. I was wrought up to a state of extreme excitement. Arthur said nothing. He took my hands quickly in his. I looked at him; his face was ghastly in its whiteness. His lips were as bloodless as his cheeks. His fingers were icy. I shrank back from him. My excitement disappeared as rapidly as it had come. I sat beside him limp and subdued.

"Elsie," said Arthur, presently, in a broken voice. "I—I must be an awful wretch."

He put his hand before his eyes; I could see the tears trickling through his slender, white fingers. My heart reproached me. Why, oh, why was I born emotional? A plague upon emotional women, one and all, say I.

"You are not—you are not," I murmured, "I am to blame after all. Don't mind what I said, dear. It is this scene, and this—this hour which have affected me. I—I could not sleep—I—"

Arthur again took my hands in his. In his eyes, as he fixed them upon my face, I saw "a something" that sent a thrill of ecstatic bliss through my heart. He leaned forward, and pressed a kiss—warm and tender—upon my lips—the first he had ever voluntarily given me. I looked up.

A cold shudder ran through my frame, a feeling of intense disgust seemed to permeate my soul. Before us stood Captain Dillington, coldly statuesque and hatefully conspicuous. Arthur dropped my hands. The flush upon his face, which I could see in the moonlight, faded. His eyes still fixed upon mine—he had not looked at the captain—grew coldly and studiously friendly as ever. The change was startling.

"I trust you do not object to my cigar, Mrs. Ravener?" asked the intruder politely.

I would rather have inhaled the smoke of ten thousand cigars lighted at one time, than listened to one word from the repulsive lips of this man.

I could not answer him. "Good-night, Arthur," I said, and rising sped across the lawn to the house, and regained my chamber. I slept.

Chapter 11

FOR eight days Captain Dillington remained with us, a most unwelcome guest as far as I was concerned. He knew it, too, I suppose. I was too young to be able to dissemble. I disliked the man so thoroughly, that I made the fact only too apparent.

My interview with Arthur in the garden, however, had eased my mind considerably. I felt now that I could soon win my way to his heart, if I could only succeed in gaining his confidence. This, I reflected, must not be forced, but carefully and studiously worked for.

Captain Dillington's visit was a source of horrible discomfort to me. To be sure, while he was in the city during the daytime, Arthur took me for a "constitutional,"[1] but after dinner I was left entirely to my own resources and those of my faithful Marie, whom I was how beginning to appreciate more than I could have thought possible. The men sat down to their detestable game of chess, and long after midnight, at which time I left them, Marie informed me that they remained at the table. When I met them at breakfast, they were polite, amiable, talkative; they seemed to think that as long as they were satisfied, all was well.

---

1   Walk.

How delighted I was when Captain Dillington at last informed me that he must return to London. I was so happy that I believe I favored him with a radiant smile, and oh, deceit! oh, hypocrisy!—hoped he would come again. I imagine he fully understood the frame of mind which induced the utterance of such a flagrantly improbable wish. I fancied I saw him bite his lips, though he merely bowed and thanked me.

"Arthur," I said, clasping my hands, while a flush of pleasure mantled my cheeks as Captain Dillington, with his valise and smile disappeared from our sight, "he has gone—at last."

Now, generally speaking, a fact that is so self-evident as the one which I had just mentioned, would need no further comment. Of course he had gone. We had seen him go. But under the circumstances it seemed to me that Arthur might have said something. He stood with his eyes fixed upon the ground, making little circles in the smooth gravel with the point of his shoe.

"Arthur, dear," I continued, laying my hand with its conspicuous gold circletted finger on his arm, "I am so glad."

My husband did not look up. "What is your objection to Captain Dillington?" he asked. "I am sure he always treated you kindly—and no one could have been more polite."

"I am jealous of him, Arthur."

I got no further in my playful remark. "How dare you talk such nonsense?" he asked, passionately, turning upon me furiously and positively glaring at me. "Women are all the same, inconsistent, foolish, unstable as water. They do not know their own minds from one moment to another. I was wrong to believe you when you declared that you would never discountenance our friendship—that you admired it—that—pshaw! what a fool I was! Great heavens! that I should have been so deceived."

"Stop!" I exclaimed, my voice ringing out so loudly that it astonished me, though I was too indignant and alarmed to pay any attention to it. "You have no right to talk in that manner to me, and I will not permit it. Captain Dillington's presence in this house was an affront to me, and he knows it if you do not. I still say I admire friendship, but when it causes a man to treat his wife with complete indifference and as a necessary incumbrance in his house, I retract and declare that I despise it—despise it from the bottom of my heart."

I turned my back upon him in silent disgust—silent, because in my bitter indignation I could say no more. Heaven knows that these angry words were called forth by himself. I would willingly have forgiven the first week of neglect and indifference, if with Captain Dillington's departure, he had shown the least sympathy for me. But to champion the cause of that intruder and disregard mine—I was no saint. He had slapped one cheek, but I would take good care that he should not slap the other.

"Have I treated you with neglect?" The anger was gone from his voice. I had frightened it away.

"Have you?" I asked scornfully. "You have treated me with such marked coldness, that even my maid, Marie, has been gossiping with the other servants about it."

Ah, I had made a mistake. I knew it the moment the words were out of my mouth.

"She has, has she?" he exclaimed in a towering rage. "She shall leave the house to-night. I will not pay a pack of drones to gossip about me. She shall go, and this minute, too."

"She shall not. If she leaves your house" (I was beside myself with rage and excitement, and was hardly accountable for what I said) "I will go too."

"Elsie!" There was actual fear in his voice. He looked so handsome as these varied emotions stirred him, that—alas! that I should say it—I felt that my indignation could not last much longer. As he uttered my name, he looked at me earnestly, and with a pained, wearied gaze. I began to feel sorry for him. Despise me, readers, and mentally declare that you would have acted far differently.

Women so often start in as plaintiffs and end as defendants in their controversies with the other sex.

"I mean it," I managed to say in a low voice.

"You would ruin my reputation," he began in a grieved tone. Unpardonably selfish as the remark was, it made just the impression upon me that he probably intended it should do.

"How can you say it?" I asked. "Arthur, listen to me. I love you, and I begin to think that I love you too well. If I did not care for you, I should be glad when you absented yourself from me, but—but—as it is—it—breaks m-my heart."

I was going to give way. I felt quite sure of that.

"Don't, Elsie," said Arthur, hastily. "Don't. I cannot stand scenes. I want you to be happy. I would not for the world see you in such distress, but—"

"But, what—"

"Nothing. Elsie, let us go for a long walk and drop these painful subjects." Painful subjects! He said it, I assure you.

"No," I said, sadly. I would not make myself cheap. He did not want me, I felt sure. I must try another policy.

"What are you going to do to pass away the morning?"

"Oh, I have a wealth of amusement," I said, smiling through my tears. "Do—do not trouble any more about me. You probably have some w-writing to do. Do not let me disturb you. Good-bye," and I ran away to my room.

Yes, I must try another policy. Perhaps I was letting him see too plainly that his neglect caused me pain. It might be that, like some men of whom I have since heard, he disliked to know that a woman was running after him. If I treated him as he treated me, perhaps I might teach him a little respect. Men do not like weak, clinging beings—at least some of them don't, and perhaps my husband belonged to that class. At any rate I would change my policy. Why do I say "change my policy"? I had none before. I was simply acting as my heart told me to act. Now I would follow the course prescribed by my reason. I could lose nothing by so doing, and I might gain my husband's love.

I congratulated myself that I had refused to accompany him on that walk. I was really dying to go, but I would deny myself the pleasure for the sake of possible results. He had not insisted—it would have been no use if he had—I told myself. Perhaps he was annoyed at my refusal. I sincerely hoped that he was. I trusted that he was even seriously angry and would resent my non-compliance with his request.

I must confess that the afternoon passed away most tediously for me. I called in Marie, and made her talk herself tired. I tried to be amused at her chatter, but I found it insufferably uninteresting. She would tell me all about Paris, and her own dull life in that city. The poor girl was the daughter of an honest little Rue du Temple *fabricant*,[1] and her history

---

1   Manufacturer.

was not exciting. If she had only been the daughter of a dishonest little *fabricant*, she would have been far more entertaining, I thought. I felt that she was supplying me with conversational gruel, and I was in a condition of mind when I wanted curry. As the hour for dinner drew nigh, I dressed myself carefully. Everything I could do to make myself look pretty—I did. I was determined that Arthur should admire me.

I recovered my spirits sufficiently to be able to "sail" downstairs, and as I reached the dining-room, the flush of excitement came to my cheeks. I wondered how it would all end. Arthur was not in the dining-room, so I threw myself into an armchair to await him. I was rather impatient. I suppose it was natural that I should be. I took up a newspaper and tried to read. I did not have to try very long.

"Mrs. Ravener." It was James, the butler. I suppose he was not sure that I was in the chair, as I was covered with newspaper.

"Yes, James."

"Master told me to give you this note."

I snatched it from the man's hands, and read it hastily. "Dear Elsie," it ran, "I have just received a telegram that calls me up to town immediately. Do not wait dinner for me, and pray do not be angry. Your affectionate husband, Arthur Ravener."

Oh, this was cruel. I waved my hand to James to dismiss him, and then flung myself upon the sofa in an agony of weeping. For twenty minutes I gave my grief full play, and then, when anger came peeping in, I let it enter and take possession of my soul. I rang the bell. James, with suspicious promptness answered the call.

"James, did any telegram come here for your master this afternoon?"

"Not to my knowledge, madame."

"Are you sure?"

"Quite."

"Go ask the servants, and find out if anybody brought a telegram for Mr. Ravener to the house to-day."

He soon returned. "No one has received any telegram. If one had come to the house," he added with the officiousness of his class, "I should have known it."

"You may go."

My blood was boiling. I would not be set aside. Perhaps Arthur Ravener thought I was a milk-and-water maiden. He made a great mistake. "I gave him the option between peace and war," I said to myself, "and he has chosen war. So be it."

I tried to be lively, but it was a failure. I was changed. I was no longer a flippant girl, but a jealous woman. Does any one know what a jealous woman really is? I think not. Perhaps a volcano always on the eve of eruption is about the best simile I can suggest.

CHAPTER 12

I AM not going to weary my readers by describing in detail the ensuing days of my married life. I adopted the new policy I had mapped out. I became apparently indifferent to my husband's presence, uninterested in his nightly outgoings and his matutinal incomings, while at the same time I treated him with studied politeness and friendly affability. We talked and laughed at the dinner-table. We discussed politics—I made it a point of disagreeing with him, for the sake of permitting him to try and win me over to his way of thinking. Of course I let him finally convince me, and then declared how foolish I must have been ever to have thought otherwise. Then we talked books—I in my superficial way, he in his earnest, well read manner. I knew the names of the authors of nearly all the popular works of the day; I was one of those airy beings who examine the covers of books, dip into catalogues, and taste literature, as it were, from the outside.

He was really so entertaining that at times I forgot I was only playing a part. I could not help thinking that he would have enjoyed the conversation just as much if it had taken place with somebody else. I suppose I seemed rather bright—some women as shallow as I was often manage to appear so. I do not believe he appreciated this brightness because it belonged to his wife, but merely—bah; I hate analysis. After all, what I believed on this subject is neither here nor there.

I made not the slightest impression upon Arthur Ravener. A month had flown by since I had stood in my dollish finery at the hymeneal altar. Our walks had been dropped. That was one of the effects of my policy. He seemed perfectly satisfied. He had evidently thought that these "constitutionals" were necessary for my happiness. If I chose to discontinue them—well, then, they were not necessary for my happiness. It was very simple after all.

At breakfast, at luncheon, and at dinner, here I was—there he was. He was as platonically kind as any man could be. He always made enquiries as to my health, my wishes, my plans. I had but to suggest a thing, and I had his acquiescence almost before I had made the suggestion. And all this time, I was eating my heart out for love of this iceberg.

Women must be contemptible things. If I were a man I suppose I could not give utterance to such an ungallant remark, but no one can find fault with me when my sex is taken into consideration, and I am quite sure I shall find plenty of sisters to agree with me.

The old adage about the woman, the dog and the hickory tree, which nicely explains that the more you beat 'em the better they'll be, seems to me wonderfully true. Why should I care for this man? I was very young, of course, but I knew perfectly well that this utter neglect was simply outrageous. I remembered my horror at the compliments and pretty speeches with which my partners in the ball-rooms of my friends had overwhelmed me. I had hated them for their silly, tinsel-bound sentiments; their ill-expressed admiration. I still did so. I should have been just as disgusted if I had heard them at the present time. But there was a happy medium to all things.

Between the conspicuously ridiculous adulation of comparative strangers, and the brotherly indifference of the man I had married, there must be a middle path of warm yet not necessarily demonstrative affection. I thought of the bride and bridegroom whom Arthur and I had criticised one night. "It disgusts me," I recollected saying, when Arthur had asked me if their conversation, to which we had listened, interested me. Well, I had no cause for such disgust in my own home. Arthur's indifference seemed to be unaffected by any policy I might adopt. I even tried to make him jealous. There was a bashful youth, who wore glasses and a perpetual smile, living close to Tavistock Villa, with an adoring mamma and two prim sisters, to whom Hector was as the apple of their eye. He had frequently cast admiringly modest glances in my direction when he had stumbled across Marie and me in our daily walks.

"*Il a l'air joliment bête*,"[1] Marie said to me once in the loud security of the French language as we passed the gallant youth. He must have thought the remark was a flattering one, because he looked even more seraphically pleasant than usual. Dasy was his surname. He lacked the *i* which would have given him some claim upon the dainty characteristics of that little flower.

Mr. Dasy amused me. The delectable idea occurred to me to use him. I would cultivate his society. I would make Arthur desperately jealous. I had always heard that those bashful, rose-colored youths were the most dangerous, and if I had heard it, surely my husband had. Who could possibly introduce us? Of course I could smile at him and encourage him that way, but I was not inclined to have recourse to the methods of an unscrupulous flirt, when I was very far from being one. How I wished that flirting came as naturally to me as it did to some women.

I could call on Mamma Dasy if I liked. Neighborly courtesy would surely sanction that, but I felt I could not do it. I had an awful idea that this mamma might patronize me. I had a hideous presentiment that she would come and see us and wonder why we were not more affectionate. I could tell by her face that she was one of those women who think it the duty of a young married couple to do a little billing and cooing *pro bono publico*.[2] I could not possibly introduce prying eyes into my strange household. I think I should have dreaded any eyes at all, at that time. I was growing morbid. Even Marie was too many for me occasionally.

Fortune favored me. One afternoon, feeling more wretched than usual, and knowing that my husband was safely shut up in his sanctum and that I should not see him until dinner time, I took up a book and strolled towards the gardens. I selected a shady spot, opened my volume, and was soon engrossed in its contents.

---

1   He has the air of an utter blockhead.

2   For the public good.

When I looked up I found that I was not alone. There, sure enough, as large as life, and equally ugly, sat the Misses Dasy—sister Euphemia and sister Sophronia. They were knitting. If they had been reading I should have looked up in surprise; if they had been drawing, my hair would have stood on end; if they had been indulging in small talk, it would have seemed indecent;—but they were knitting. It looked so natural. They belonged to the knitting class of females. As I said, I looked up. I smiled. Sister Sophronia smiled. Sister Euphemia smiled. We all smiled.

"How strange we do not meet more frequently, Mrs. Ravener," quoth sister Euphemia. "Hector says he often comes across you and your maid." "Yes," chirped sister Sophronia, "we wondered why we so rarely met you."

I thanked the stars—mentally, of course—that I had not been inflicted before. Now, however, I was rather glad to see them, as by them I might find access to dear Hector. So I told no fib when I remarked that I was charmed, though I am afraid that I should not have permitted a fib or two to stand in my way if they could have done me any good.

"Mr. Ravener does not believe in country walks, I suppose," remarked Euphemia presently, "like most men," she added.

Hateful sister Euphemia! I am convinced that her acquaintance with men must have been limited to dear Hector, and—as Portia says—God made him, so let him pass as a man.[1]

"Hush, Euphemia," said Sophronia in an audible aside, and in a virtuous tone. She could not have made any remark less calculated to please me. It was evident they had been discussing us.

"My husband is a literary man and writes all day long," said I, with one of the serenest, most child-like and fancy-picture smiles I had ever conjured up. "I dislike to disturb him, you know. Men are such queer things, are they not?"

"Yes," laughed Sophronia girlishly.

"Indeed they are," simpered Euphemia, dropping a stitch as a punishment for her giddiness.

"Is your brother a literary man?" I asked boldly.

"Oh, no," said Sophronia, scornfully, "dear Hector is nicely established in the hop business—malt and hops, you know." (Evidently imagining

---

1   *The Merchant of Venice* (I.i.55-56).

that I might think he was a dancing master). "He is taking a holiday just now. He has been working so hard. Dear Hector!"

"He admires you, Mrs. Ravener," quoth Euphemia. "He says you have a face like a woman in—in—some painting, I can't remember the name."

Great goodness! Perhaps he referred to one of the paintings given away with a pound of tea. She was so vague, that fond sister.

"Mr. Dasy compliments me," I said artlessly. "Do you know I think he is a very interesting looking young man. Hector you said his name was? Ah, it is not a misnomer." I sighed just a little.

I felt they always told Hector everything. I was convinced that my utterances would be repeated unembellished. We chatted on pleasantly for half an hour. I made myself as nice as I possibly could, and I think I succeeded in impressing them favorably, I reserved my master-stroke for my departure.

"Good-bye, dear Miss Sophronia—good-bye, dear Miss Euphemia," I said gushingly, as I rose to go. "I am so delighted to have met you. You must call upon me" (I had to say it). "I have enjoyed this afternoon hugely. The gardens are certainly charming. I really think I shall come every day this week, beginning with to-morrow—" this with a little affected chirrup which might signify that I did not really mean it.

Ah, they would tell Hector, and he would accompany them to-morrow. For a beginner in the fashionable art of diplomacy, I was not so bad after all. They looked admiringly after me as I went, and I felt that they would gaze in my direction long after I could see them.

I was formally introduced to Mr. Dasy the following day. The modest hop merchant was completely overwhelmed. He grew purple in the face at everything I said for the first quarter of an hour, which means that his countenance was tinged with that royal hue during the entire fifteen minutes, for he allowed me to do all the talking. I did not flirt. I tried to do so, but could not succeed. I spoke sensibly, flattered Mr. Dasy a little—if that does not give discredit to my statement that I spoke sensibly—and simply allowed him to see that I liked talking to him. Hector certainly was not given to flattery.

He told me all about hops, the magnificent prospects for next year, how last year's crop had been anything but a good one; how terribly small the profits were in these times of cut-throat competition, and similar edifying facts. His talk was hoppy in the extreme. I felt that if only I could have talked malt the combination would have lulled us into beery intoxication.

For a week I cultivated the society of Hector Dasy. I should have been bored to death if I had not kept my object in view. I walked him up and down the Branston Road, in front of the windows of Tavistock Villa. I knew Arthur saw us at least twice, but he said nothing at all.

He was just as amiably indifferent when I met him at dinner; he spoke just as entertainly; not by the faintest indication on his part, was I hurting him. Branston Road only possessed about half a dozen extremely detached houses, so I was not at all afraid of the neighbors. If the thoroughfare, however, had been densely lined with tenements, I do not think it would have made the least difference in my course of action.

At last I resolved upon a final stroke. If it did not succeed I would drop Mr. Dasy, perfectly convinced that I could never make Arthur jealous. It was rather a risky thing to do. I asked Hector Dasy to bring me a book that I particularly wanted, and kept him during the entire afternoon, my willing slave. Before this, I told James to give Mr. Ravener's letters into my possession and to inform his master, as soon as he came in, that I had them. I did this merely in order that Arthur should be forced to enter the drawing-room and see how nicely Hector Dasy and I agreed.

Never had any afternoon passed so slowly for me. The presence of this young man annoyed me intensely and all the more because in order to keep him, I was forced to talk prettily and incessantly. Mr. Dasy was something of a coxcomb with all his bashfulness. I saw with alarm that he really imagined I liked him. I wondered what he would have said if I had told him the true facts of the case. Just before six o'clock, which was my husband's time for returning from town, when he passed the day there, I completed my Macchiavellianism.[1] I had purchased a quantity of wool, which I wanted wound. I was determined that Mr. Dasy should hold it for me. I made him kneel on

---

1   Niccolò Machiavelli (1469-1527), Italian political philosopher, whose posthumously published *The Prince* (1532) is a brutally realist treatise on the exercise of political power.

the rug before me, and at six o'clock I was winding for dear life, and he was smiling beatifically.

Ah! I heard Arthur's step at last. I could always recognize it. James was telling him that I had his letters. James had told. He was coming in my direction. The door opened. He entered.

Now for my *rôle*. "Arthur," I said with affected hesitation, "let me introduce you to my friend, Mr. Dasy—Mr. Dasy, my husband, Mr. Ravener."

I watched Arthur's face. I did not dare to look at poor Mr. Dasy. My husband's countenance showed positively no change. "I am glad to meet you, Mr. Dasy," he began. "I see you are making yourself useful. Isn't it rather too much to ask visitors to assist in such a laborious operation as wool-winding, Elsie?" he said, smiling at me in all good fellowship, perfectly satisfied as though Hector had been Marie or—not to libel my French maid by comparison—a dummy from a tailor's shop.

"Mr. Dasy has been here idling away the afternoon," I said as lightly as I could, "and I thought I would utilize his services."

"Delighted, I'm sure," put in poor Hector, who had been looking for his tongue and had only just found it.

"You have my letters, have you not, Elsie?" asked Arthur, coming at once to business.

"Yes," I said coldly, "I took them because I thought they—er—looked—er—important," lamely.

Hector Dasy soon found an opportunity to go. Of course he knew I had a husband, but I presume he had not reckoned upon an introduction while wool-winding. Poor Hector! I felt a little guilty, or should have done if I had given myself the time.

"Dasy seems a nice young fellow, Elsie," said Arthur coolly, at dinner that night. "His family have lived in Kew for years. Eminently respectable. Old Dasy left them well off. I am glad you have discovered congenial society among our neighbors, Elsie," looking at me in such a friendly, disinterested fashion, that I shuddered. "You are mistress here, dear, and you can ask as many people to Tavistock Villa as you like. I shall never interfere."

Of that I now felt certain. Well, my plot had been an utter and a dismal failure. All my time had been spent for nothing. I had cultivated this nonentity with an object in view. The nonentity was there in all his cultivation, and the object had disappeared. I could never make my husband jealous.

What could I do? Tavistock Villa was becoming disgusting to me. I could not endure its atmosphere much longer. I would go up to London to-morrow, make a confidant of my mother—a thing I had never yet done—and hear what she thought about the situation.

CHAPTER 13

YOU, my fair young readers, will imagine that nothing could be easier than to go to your mother, and tell her—well, anything on earth. That is because you have the right kind of a mother. I had the wrong kind. I am well aware that such a sentiment is not pretty from anybody's lips, but as you already know, I am one of those candid beings who conceal nothing, even when concealment might be beneficial.

There had never been any confidence between my mother and me. She had always considered me uninteresting, and I—well, I could never realize that she really existed out of society. Her ambition never extended beyond the "set" in which she moved; her ideas were suggested invariably by those immediately above her in rank; worldliness reigned rampant within her.

I had been glad to leave her house, and rejoiced to escape from society's prospective thraldom. And now I was going to consult my mother on a question of vital importance. I was about to appeal to the very worldliness which I condemned, to assist me in my dilemma.

I had no difficulty in leaving Tavistock Villa for London. I do not suppose that if I had set out for Timbuctoo, any very unconquerable obstacles would have presented themselves.

My journey to town was without incident; my arrival at Grosvenor Square, stupid. The butler was far too well bred to express any surprise when he beheld me; the maids whom I met *en route* to my mother's morning-room, were too well drilled in fashionable idiocy to look either pleased or interested when I burst upon them.

My mother had only just risen. She had been at an ultra-swell reception the night before, and was to be present at another that evening, so that the interval between the two was to be spent in a lounge-chair with a novel and a few newspapers—those that chronicled in detail the events of society.

She pressed a farcical kiss upon my brow, said she was charmed to see me—though she wasn't—wondered why I had come in such an informal manner and so disgracefully soon, hoped dear Arthur was well, and—well, would I not sit down, and take off my cloak?

I unbosomed myself without any delay. I did not attempt to shield Arthur's neglect. I felt that he deserved everything I could say—and more. I did not tell my mother that I was miserable, because my ideas of misery and happiness did not coincide with hers. I simply laid the situation before her, and asked her superior knowledge of the world what it all meant.

Her languor disappeared as I proceeded; she even sat up straight in her lounge-chair, and when I came to an end she deliberately closed her novel—a tacit recognition of the fact that I was more entertaining than her author.

"Well, my dear," she said blandly, when I paused, "this story is strange indeed, but—but singularly interesting."

"Interesting?" I asked, horrified.

"Yes, my dear, certainly interesting. Though I always thought Arthur Ravener a peculiar young man—you remember when I saw you two in the library that day—I never supposed that he suffered from anything but bashfulness. Bashfulness, though a grievous fault in these enlightened days when young men are supposed to have overcome any little *gaucheries*[1] long before they attain their majority, is not an unsurmountable objection. You see what I mean? I always thought—you know, Elsie, I do a great deal of thinking in my quiet way—that you and he would settle down

---

1   Awkwardness.

into a commonplace, everyday couple. Not for one instant did any idea to the contrary enter my head."

She was gratified. I could see it. With disgust in my soul, and no very filial reverence written upon my unpleasantly mobile features, I was obliged to realize the fact that this society mother was entertained by the story of her daughter's marital misfortunes.

"It was only the other day," she went on, "that I heard that Lady Erminow's daughter who was recently married to that young scapegrace, Erickson—you remember her, Elsie, that pretty golden-haired girl—was living so unhappily with her husband. He is a slave to alcohol, my dear. Nothing could be worse than that. It is the lowest, most degrading passion. Lady Erminow has my heartfelt sympathy. By-the-bye, Elsie, Arthur, you omitted to tell me—is he abstemious?"

"Yes—as far as I know," I answered, bitterly.

"I thought it," said my mother, triumphantly. "The cause of his neglect must be found elsewhere. Do not worry yourself at all, Elsie."

"What do you mean?" I asked excitedly. "Do you think you know why he neglects me?"

My mother looked at me with intense scorn. "Of course I do. Do you suppose I have lived so long in the world without being able to diagnose this simple case of domestic infelicity. My dear Elsie, another girl of your age would not need aid in this matter. The case is absolutely transparent. Husband indifferent, always away from home, uninterested in wife—why, my dear child, it is all as plain as a pikestaff."

I listened eagerly. If I only understood the situation I had no doubt but that I could grapple with it. How glad I felt that I had come. If I knew the malady, surely I could find the remedy.

"One thing—before I proceed, Elsie," continued my mother, now so interested that her novel fell to the ground unheeded. "Your case would not be considered at all strange in society, and rest assured, dear, that you would not suffer in the least. Society is a kind friend—my best,—as I have told you so often. Still for the present I do not think I would ventilate my grievances, if I were you—"

"What do you mean?" I interrupted indignantly.

"Hear me, Elsie, and do not be so impulsive, please. As I was saying, for the present I would not ventilate my grievances, as in such a very young married couple, they might—remember I say 'might'—cause a little comment. If you had been married twelve months, or even six—yes, I think six," she added, reflectively, "I would not caution you thus. You see—"

"Nothing," I exclaimed, angrily, "you explain nothing."

"If you do not understand the case," continued my mother, looking rather keenly at me, "perhaps it would be better for your interests—and mine, for I am your mother, Elsie—that you should not do so. Live quietly for a few months more, and then—"

"I will not!" I cried, rising energetically from my seat. "I will not endure such a home, unless there be some very excellent reason why I should do so. I love my husband—I may as well tell you that; but when I see myself neglected in such a shameful way, through nothing that I have done, I will not submit blindly to it. Tell me what the cause of this trouble is, if you know, and I will try to remedy it. If I can do so, and can gain Arthur's love, no one will be happier than I. If I cannot, I will leave him, before the—the—whole affair k-kills me."

I burst into tears.

"You are unreasonably excited," said my mother, sternly, "or you would not dare to talk to me of leaving your husband. Why, girl, your position would be gone—and mine too. You talk of suffering through no fault of your own, but you seem extremely willing to let me suffer through no fault of mine. If you left your husband, I might as well close my establishment. All London would talk, and I—I pride myself upon furnishing no food for idle and detrimental gossip."

She rose from her seat and walked up and down the room, thoroughly and selfishly roused.

"Why will you not take my advice?" she asked. "Go home and stay there quietly for a few months. Then I will tell you what to do."

"I will not!" I exclaimed passionately.

My mother reflected. She saw that I was determined. I was. As I sat in that room I resolved that if I could not discover the cause of my husband's coldness—and discovering, vanquish it—I would leave my married life forever.

"If you will not," said my mother, after a good two minutes of complete silence, and in a wisely calculating tone, "something must be done. Of course, Elsie, there's a woman in the case."

A woman in the case! What woman? What did my mother mean?

"The expression is not a pretty one," resumed my parent, taking my surprise for ladylike wonder at the construction of her phrase. "But it means everything. You know, Elsie, that the French in every catastrophe that happens, declare that *'cherchez la femme'*[1] will explain everything."

"I do not understand you," I said in a dazed way. "Why there is not a soul in our house but the servants and my maid, Marie."

"Perhaps not," said Mrs. Bouverie. "But there are plenty of souls out of your house, my dear, and—according to your story—that is where your husband spends the greater part of his time. His neglect of you is only too clear. He is interested in some other woman, and with her he spends his time. Have I made myself clear?"

She had. I started up, surprised at my own obtuseness and burning to settle this question once and forever. But—no, I could not understand fully.

"If he is interested in some other woman," I asked helplessly, "why did he marry me? He asked me to be his wife. Nobody forced him to do it. I didn't suggest it."

My mother laughed harshly. "I suppose not," she said. "Perhaps he wanted you to be his wife on account of the superior social advantages a married man enjoys. Perhaps as a married man his liaison could be carried on more favorably. Perhaps—there are a hundred suggestions I could make. Don't let us forget the fact, also, that you were dowered handsomely."

"Nonsense; he did not want my money, be quite sure of that. Mother," I said, putting on my cloak and buttoning it all wrong, "you are right, there is a woman in the case, and I was blind not to have seen it."

"No doubt your husband's friend, the Captain, is the go-between. That might explain his intimacy with your husband, might it not?"

Of course it might.

"Yes," I said. "What would you advise me to do?"

"I suppose you ask that," said mamma, severely, "in order that you may do something else. You are too obstinate, too self-willed to ask advice. Still," seeing that I looked threatening—I must have done so for I am sure I felt it—"perhaps I had better make a suggestion or two. Go

---

1   Look for the woman.

home to your husband and tax him with his infidelity; you will easily see by his manner if the shot strikes home. Don't be impulsive and—ridiculous—as you generally are. Try a little diplomacy. If your husband denies everything—come to me, and I'll help you with a detective or two."

"I will," I said promptly.

"And now, go, Elsie," sinking wearily into her chair, "I declare you have fatigued me. I shall never be able to get through the reception—all this on top of my fatigues of last night."

She waved me away. I did not offer her my brow to freeze. I could not.

Her words rang in my ears all the way home. "A woman in the case." Yes, of course there must be. What a bat I must have been not to have suspected it before. I was eccentric. There was no doubt about it. I ought to have waited a few years before I had married, and gained a little experience in the world. But no! If the price of such experience was the forfeit of my self-respect, I did not want it.

A woman in the case! Who could she be? I wondered if she were more attractive than I was. What a fool I had been to imagine that he would notice me, as I strutted before my glass in the silly pride of a peacock! He was all the time thinking of some one else. I wondered why I could not picture this "some one else." I seemed utterly unable to realize the fact that Arthur Ravener could love another woman.

However, my future should soon be decided. I was excited, earnest, and eager to begin my self-imposed task.

CHAPTER 14

T HE strength of my resolution to arrive at a definite comprehension of the situation in which I found myself, acted in a sort of sedative manner upon my unstrung nerves. Though I raged during the ride from Grosvenor Square to Kew, at the end of my journey I was calm; desperately calm.

I dressed for dinner with just as much care as usual, and though I did not "frivol" before the glass, and think what an attractive little lady I was, I omitted nothing in my *toilette* that could render me more comely.

I found Arthur in the dining-room when I entered that gloomy apartment, and we greeted each other in just the same friendly, platonic manner that had ever marked our demeanor towards one another. We sat opposite to one another at the long table, and I prepared myself for my usual hour of small talk upon the theatres, the latest pictures, the political situation, and a variety of other topics.

I could feel no interest in anything, however. Horrible visions of Arthur, my husband, *tête-à-tête* with another woman, would fill my brain to the exclusion of everything else; disgust at my husband's deceit; contempt for my own inability to please him; wonder as to how it would all end, and a bewildering attempt to remember everything I had planned to say, played havoc with my conversational powers.

Yes, I was outrageously jealous—blindly, hatefully jealous, with the jealousy which Sardou loves to imagine and Bernhardt[1] to portray, and though I was by no means dramatically inclined, I felt that my situation was unusual. I tried to prolong the meal. I was determined to "have it out," as the saying is, and yet I dreaded the process, because I felt that Arthur must be guilty. I knew I should feel sorry for him. He was one of those few men who could make you pity him at the same time that he cut your throat, and I was one of those many women in whom unnatural compassion exists in all its power.

Dinner was over. I could not prolong it any further if I tried. He had risen from the table. He was about to leave me—"Arthur." I swallowed a lump. My voice sounded choked.

"Elsie," he said, turning at once, and coming back to me. He stood and looked in my face with the cool, un-ardent friendship which I hated to see there. "What is it?"

He waited patiently while I gulped again and strove to be cool.

"May I speak to you, Arthur?"

He laughed.

"Why, Elsie, have you not been speaking to me for the last hour. I always like to hear you, dear. You are one of the most thoroughly sensible little women I have ever met. I—"

"Don't!" I cried, with a gesture of disgust. "Spare me. I do not want to discuss the newspapers, or talk pretty nothings, I wish to speak with you—quietly, you know—on a—a serious matter, con-connected only with ours-selves. Will you come into my sitting-room? Don't—be—afraid. I—I—will not k-keep you l-long."

My teeth chattered in my head with nervousness. I felt cold. My husband looked more uncomfortable than I did. He fidgetted with his feet. His lips twitched slightly. Oh, he knew what was coming as well as I did.

"Will you come?" I repeated as he stood mute and uneasy before me.

"Of course," with an effort, "if you wish it."

1   Victorien Sardou (1831-1908), French playwright; Sarah Bernhardt (1844-1923), famous French actress.

If I wished it? I bore him off to my sitting-room. He had never entered the apartment before with me, except when he first introduced me to it. I closed the door. He waited until I took an arm-chair by the window. Then he quietly sat down at the other end of the room and picked up a book. His evident fear that I was about to become demonstrative, while it cut me to the quick, was not without its ridiculous side.

"Ha! Ha!" I laughed hysterically, "you need not be afraid. I won't kiss you. I've not brought you here to tell you how I love you; that would not be original enough to please you—or me. Ha! Ha! Ha!"

I threw myself back in my chair and laughed until the tears rolled down my face. I felt the acutest anguish—and still I laughed. My heart was harrowed by this man's neglect and contempt—and still I laughed. I could not help it. I suppose it was a physiological peculiarity.

Finally I covered my face in my hands and sobbed convulsively.

"Elsie," cried Arthur in the greatest alarm, "you are ill. What is the matter? I" (rising) "will go for Dr. White."

He wanted to get out of the room. If he did, I should see him no more that day. He reckoned without his host.

"I want no doctor," I declared, rising and standing with my back to the door, all hysteria vanished. "If I do, James shall go, and you can remain here with me. I—I know you will like that."

Again I laughed long and passionately. I was becoming exhausted by this most exhausting emotion. Great goodness! I must make an effort. Here the minutes were slipping quickly by and I had not accomplished a thing. My rival was yet unknown to me.

"Excuse me, Arthur," I said quietly, after a long pause in which he paced the floor uneasily, "your experience with women," I looked him keenly in the face, "will tell you that I—I—am—am—out of sorts."

"What do you mean, Elsie?"

No one could have better feigned surprise I told myself. Arthur Ravener must be an accomplished actor. There was the genuine astonishment, caused by a revelation, upon his face.

"You know what I mean," I answered.

"I do not. I swear it."

"You do," I cried, trying unsuccessfully not to ruin my cause by bitter denunciation. "You do"—more quietly. I walked over to him, grasped his arm, and looked into his face. "Now," I said, "tell me honestly, and as a man, that you do not know what I mean."

He shook me off. He was growing angry. "I will tell you nothing," he said, not glancing at me, "until you have explained yourself."

"Very well. Listen. When a young girl marries a man who a few hours after the wedding leaves her alone in a strange house; who makes a lame excuse for his action and subsequently increases his offense against respect and affection by permitting her to pass her time in absolute solitude; who for love substitutes the coldest and most indifferent friendship; who spends a large part of his time in town, leaving her in the country, and attempts no sort of explanation—when he does all this, what is she to suspect?"

He had been growing paler while I put the questions, but as I concluded he started up in undisguised fear—yes, it was fear.

"Suspect?" he asked, hoarsely. "What right have you to suspect anything? All shame upon the education of girls to-day, if a child like you dares to suspect."

He was as white as a sheet and unreasonably angry.

"You are an excellent diplomat," I said satirically. "You knew too well what a child I was when you married me. The extent of my knowledge of good and evil had been very well gauged by you. I have suspected nothing, and you know it. But, thank Heaven, my blindness has been cured. I can see it all now."

"You have been gossiping," he exclaimed, glaring at me.

"I have done nothing of the kind. I have been neglected and humiliated. I knew no reason why this state of things should exist, so—I asked my mother's advice."

The shot struck home. Arthur Ravener gasped for breath. He seemed absolutely unable to speak.

"You—asked—your—mother's—advice," he managed to articulate, presently. "And—what—did—she—tell—you?"

"She told me this, and I confront you with it: that there was undeniable proof in your neglect that you cared nothing for me, except as a sort of respectable cloak, but that there must be another woman whom you loved, and whom you visited when you were not at Tavistock Villa."

"Ah!"

If I had not known that such a thing must be impossible I should have imagined that Arthur's exclamation was one of relief. The expression of his face changed at once from one of intense alarm to comparative composure. He took a seat, leaned his elbows on his knees, covered his face with his hand, and remained silent.

"Why do you not speak?" I asked impatiently.

"Listen, Elsie," drawing closer to me. "I will be brief. Years ago I vowed I would never marry; you may think that was a boyish resolve. It was not; I thoroughly meant it, as a man. The reason was that women were too exacting, though a house without a woman in it was and still is to me a terribly lonely, uninteresting place. I resolved never to marry. I met you. As you say very justly, I studied you carefully. I came to the conclusion that you were unlike other girls—that we would live quietly and happily together as friends—you going your way and I going mine. I say I firmly believed that this could be done when I married you. I esteemed you greatly, and, Elsie," he paused for a moment, "my esteem has been increased tenfold. Lately, however, it has seemed to me that our life was becoming distasteful to you. At first I thought nothing of the symptoms, but I was unable to think thus lightly of them, later. Elsie," his voice quivering with emotion, "suppose we have made a great mistake?"

For a few moments I was bewildered. His argument was made in such a pathetic tone, that I felt unnatural compassion for him at the expense of my own womanliness would ruin the situation, if I were not on my guard.

"I do not understand you," I said. "You have not answered my mother's suggestions. If—if you love another woman, make a clean breast of it to me—your wife, and oh, Arthur," melting in spite of myself, "I—I will try to—to forgive you the wrong you have done me."

I seized his hand in a frenzy of grief. If only he would tell me all, everything could be remedied, I felt sure.

"Who is the woman?" I asked boldly.

He made no answer.

"Tell me who she is and all shall be set right."

He smiled at me pitifully, "She does not exist," he said. "Elsie, you are the only woman in the world to me."

I recoiled from him in disgust. "You are equivocating," I said sternly "Be frank while there is still time."

"I am frank," he said in a choked voice.

"Swear that you are telling me the truth."

"I swear it."

I arose. The numbness of despair was upon me. My suffering was deadened, my nerves were lulled into temporary quietude. There was nothing further needed. He had lied to me. I knew that. I had been so blind, that the light shed upon me by my mother's revelation seemed twenty times more powerful to me than if it had not come upon me so suddenly.

"Thank you," I said, opening the door. "Let me apologize for having detained you so long. Good-night."

He had nothing more to say. He passed out of the room, without one glance in my direction.

CHAPTER 15

THE months dragged themselves slowly away as though they hated to go, but would infinitely prefer to remain and gloat over my misery. I could not make up my mind to confer with my mother again. Although she had told me she would aid me, I seemed unable to pluck up the courage to know the worst.

My life at Tavistock Villa was unchanged. My relations with my husband were colder than ever. Though never once did he allude to the subject of the conversation recorded in the last chapter, I could see that it had made an impression upon him. He looked at me wistfully; our conversation was strained; a horrible form had stepped in between us, assuming shape as definitely as did the geni in the Arabian Nights story, from a mere shadow.

You would think that his course of action would have been changed. Not a bit of it. We met as before at breakfast and at dinner, after which he would leave the house. He never attempted any explanation, and I, always on the eve of desperate measures, maintained an equally guarded silence.

Of course I was in Grosvenor Square frequently during those wretched days, but as I did not allude to my misfortunes, my mother, selfishly afraid of a scandal which might endanger her eminently respectable position in the society which she loved a great deal better than she did her soul, made no effort to ascertain the situation of affairs.

I suppose my husband and I might have lived together pleasantly. There are women in this world—I have met a few of them—who have occupied similar positions with a smile on their faces. I could not do it. I was not a humbug, I was sorry to say. If only young girls were forced to study the elements of humbuggery as a part of an academic curriculum, what a quantity of subsequent suffering some of them would be spared! The study might be absolutely necessary to only a few, but it would be of benefit to all.

My cup of anguish was full when I met Letty Bishop—married and wonderfully happy. Dear me! How she loved that husband of hers. I compared her affection for dear Reginald to mine for Arthur Ravener, and then stopped. Her husband returned her love with interest. There never was a better mated couple.

I met them at my mother's house one evening. Arthur was with me for the sake of appearances, I suppose. How he ever managed to tear himself away from HER I could not imagine. I did not ask him for any information on the subject.

"What a happy couple!" I said with a sigh. I could not help the remark. Arthur was beside me. I was sitting, like an antique, faded wallflower in the drawing-room, while the others talked and chatted and laughed and gossiped at the other end of the room. He followed my eyes and saw Reginald talking in a whisper to Letty, while a pink-faced maiden executed a *morceau* on the piano.

"They are very impolite to talk while Miss Lancaster is playing," he said coldly.

"They have so much to say," I suggested.

"Doubtless."

"We shall never be troubled with such a burning desire to speak," I went on scornfully.

"That is your fault. I am always willing to talk with you. I enjoy talking with you, Elsie. You are unhappy, and it grieves me sorely to know it—because—because—I am helpless. Our marriage was a—a—mistake. You will not make the best of it. You are eating your heart away with worry. I would give all I possess to have it otherwise."

"You must imagine," I said sternly, "that I am either a lunatic or an idiot, otherwise you would not talk to me so senselessly."

"I imagine nothing of the kind."

"Then you did when you married me?"

"I did not. I thought, as we said so often, that you were in earnest when you declared you would be satisfied with quiet friendship instead of impetuous passion—"

"Then, as you imagine you were mistaken, you propose allowing matters to remain as they are."

"I do not see what else to do. Elsie, why need we quarrel? I esteem you. I admire you. I am sorry—"

"Thank you very much," I said bitterly. "You are very kind. You do me a great honor. You esteem me. You admire me. Oh, that is charming of you. Could you not have esteemed me and admired me without this nonsense?" pointing to my wedding ring. I would have flung it from the open window before us, only I, too, had appearances to keep up.

He made no answer, and I left him, going over to my friend Letty, and permitting her to pour her rhapsodies into my ears. She enjoyed the process immensely, and—well, I could just stand it, and that is about all.

Before I left my mother's house my mind was made up. I would dillydally no longer. I would accept my mother's aid, and settle matters finally. I was, as Arthur said, eating out my heart, and it would be better to act while there was still something left of it. I would see my mother on the following morning, and before I returned to Kew I would know that my "case" was in hands that would dispose of it satisfactorily.

I did not sleep at all that night, but with the ever faithful Marie by my side "killed time" as best I could. Marie was a good girl, but like most of her class, officious. She thought it quite correct to openly sympathize with me, and declare that *monsieur* treated his wife shamefully. This irritated me, and, if anything, made me still more fretfully anxious.

I was in Grosvenor Square early the following morning, and burst into my mother's room while she was putting a little suspicion of something rosy upon her face.

"Good gracious me, Elsie!" she exclaimed in amazed vexation, as I threw myself into a chair, "you should indeed cultivate a little repose. You really alarm me with your impulsive movements."

I made no answer. I was not in a humor for repartee of any kind. I waited as quietly as I could while mamma hurried a little china dish containing red out of sight, fondly imagining, I suppose, that I had not seen it. Then she sat down with a hectic flush on one side of her face.

"Domestic troubles, of course," she said, satirically.

"Of course," I replied, with equal satire.

"Well?"

"You said you would help me when I needed your services. I need them now," I replied.

My mother meditated. I could see that she was unwilling to assist me. She dreaded anything happening which might give the matter publicity. In a word, she was afraid of me, and I admit, not without reason.

"I do not like interfering between man and wife," she began tentatively.

But I was equal to the occasion. The avalanche had started on its course, and nothing could now stop it.

"Very well," I said with palpably assumed indifference, "if you will not aid me in a matter concerning my happiness, I shall leave my husband at once."

As I said, my indifference was palpably assumed, but my mother was one of those who cannot see a pin's point below the surface. The random shot took effect.

"You will do nothing of the kind," she said, severely. "I beg of you, Elsie, to do nothing rash. You will bring my gray hairs with sorrow to the grave," tearfully.

She had employed that expression ever since I could remember, and its dramatic force was impaired by old age. When I used to spoil my frocks at school, when I said rude things, when I insulted my governess, or when I overdrew my weekly allowance—errors with which she was always made acquainted—I was ever threatened with bringing her gray hairs in sorrow to the grave.

She walked to her *secretaire*, and sat down. Then, taking a sheet of note paper with a crest and monogram of enormous proportions, she scribbled a few lines in a bold, back-hand. Folding the sheet, she placed it in a heavily monogrammed envelope, which she left open as she handed it to me. It was addressed to Octavius Rickaby, Esq., Holborn Viaduct.

"Go there," she said, shortly.

"Who is Octavius Rickaby?" I asked feebly.

My mother smiled contemptuously. "Of course you wouldn't know," she said. "Mr. Rickaby is a very clever private detective—or rather the head of an admirably conducted private detective office. He conducts a great many society cases"—sinking her voice to a whisper—"in fact I could name several of my friends whom he has helped. Of course, Elsie, if you make a fool of yourself, and fail to put him in possession of every detail of your case—every detail, mind—you must not be surprised if he fails. If you make a confidant of him, he will be of very material assistance, in fact your husband will not be able to wink unless you know it. He is reasonable, and, my dear, he is perfectly upright. He will never trouble you after you have settled his bill."

My heart sank within me. The word detective had an awful significance in my mind. In fact, I think I would as soon have invoked the aid of Mephistopheles.[1] Detectives always suggested murders and abductions and burglaries to me. A great many people will doubtless sympathize with this feeling.

My mother was "eyeing" me. "You do not intend to consult Mr. Rickaby, I see plainly," she said. "You will be sorry for it one of these days."

She might be right. After all, a detective might be of great service, and something must be done. "I will see Mr. Rickaby, and at once," I declared, rising with determination. "I am much obliged to you, mother. I am sorry to have disturbed you," I said, really becoming cheerful as I resolved upon immediate action; "I know I am an awful nuisance. Now go on with your dressing." I meant painting, but accuracy at times is detestable.

I drove at once to Mr. Rickaby's office in Holborn Viaduct, and was soon in front of a large glass door with the words "Octavius Rickaby" in gleaming black letters staring me in the face. I did not dare to stop and think for one moment. I walked straight in, just as my excitement, born of my eagerness to act, was wearing away like the effect of a much abused

---

1   A demon or devil in German folklore, to whom the scholar Faust sells his soul for unlimited knowledge.

drug. I found myself in a neat little office, comfortably furnished, and not at all murderous or penny-dreadful[1] looking. A polite young clerk, in a blue tie and a jovial face, which he seemed perpetually endeavoring to harmonize with the solemnity of his position, received me.

"Please take my card and this letter to Mr. Rickaby," I said, trying to appear as indifferent as though it were part of the daily routine of my life to consult with private detectives.

Of course I expected to be kept waiting. I ignorantly classed detectives with doctors and lawyers and editors, who are always "very busy just now," or if they are not, they pretend to be for the sake of appearances. I was agreeably surprised when Mr. Rickaby said he would see me at once. No, there could be no humbug about that man.

The great Octavius was stout and rubicund—another favorable point with me. No one could have looked less mysterious, and more matter of fact. I believe I half expected to enter his presence with an "open sesame," and to behold two or three imps of darkness skipping about with a caldron between them. He rose as I entered, placed a chair for me, and leaned back in his own cosy, cushioned seat.

"Tell me everything, Mrs. Ravener," said Mr. Rickaby suavely, "no one comes to see me unless he has something to tell. Consider me your doctor or your lawyer. Explain your case, and I will diagnose it."

He said all this in rather a fragmentary manner, expecting me to begin, and uttering each new sentence as he noticed that I remained silent.

He encouraged me by his patience and well-bred demeanor. I told him my story,—at least as much as I could of it. I omitted the fact that Arthur left me a few hours after our wedding. Mr. Rickaby remained silent for some moments after I had finished. Then he asked me if I had taxed Arthur with neglect. I told him I had done so in a very vigorous manner.

"You suspect that you have a rival?" he asked, looking at me keenly.

"What am I to think?"

"Have you ever discovered any letters or papers in your husband's possession that would lead you to such a belief?"

"I have not tried to discover any," I said.

---

1   Popular in the nineteenth century, "penny dreadfuls" were cheap paperback publications that contained serialized stories of a lurid or violent nature.

"Will you do so?"

I promised that I would, but begged him not to wait for any possible discoveries on my part before he began proceedings in the matter.

"You have not told me everything, Mrs. Ravener." Mr. Rickaby said this with such an air of certainty that I was dumfounded. He had not removed his eyes from my face during the progress of my story, or during the time he had interrogated me.

"I have told you all—all I—I can tell you," I said in a low tone, averting my head. Still those eagle eyes were rivetted upon me. They seemed to burn into my soul. I was disconcerted and rose hastily.

"Do not stare at me so," I said angrily, walking to the window.

"I beg your pardon, Mrs. Ravener," he remarked quietly, "I am sorry to annoy you. Sit down." I sat down. "You know," playing musingly with a paper-knife, "I often have customers who tell me all they can—like you," he said, "so I have to adopt other means to learn the information withheld. I read it in their faces."

"Then—?" I began furiously.

"You need not trouble to tell me any more," he said quietly. "It is not necessary."

I cannot describe my sensations. They were too painful to be recognizable in pen and ink. My face burned and my lips were parched. I was almost sorry I had come. But the worst was over, and I must bring this loathsome interview to an end.

"Do you think that—that," I hated to use the horrible expression that I had heard from my mother's lips—"there is a woman in—in the case?"

"It is possible," he said indefinitely.

"Possible!" I echoed in surprise. "What do you mean?"

"Mrs. Ravener," said Mr. Rickaby, "I will not express an opinion; I have no right to do so. I will possess myself of all the information I can. I will find out where your husband goes."

"You will?" I exclaimed joyfully. "Then, Mr. Rickaby, if you will do that you can leave the rest to me. Just find out for me where he goes, and I will then see what it will be best for me to do. Leave me to discover who the woman is. I—I should like to know—exclusively."

I told the truth. I did not want even a detective to possess himself of all my husband's secrets. To my surprise Mr. Rickaby seemed relieved.

"You will do this," I asked, "without going any farther?"

"Most willingly," he replied, "I will obey your instructions to the letter. It is to my interest to do so." That satisfied me.

CHAPTER 16

I RETURNED quietly home—that is to say, I was quiet when I reached Tavistock Villa. The interval between my departure from the office of Mr. Octavius Rickaby and my arrival in Kew was spent in the tedious process of schooling myself to be what I was not, and never could be—cold and stony. I felt that everything depended upon the systematic manner in which I conducted my investigation. If I gave the reins to my impulsiveness, I knew I should ruin my case.

My case! How I hated the sound of the words. The love I had brought to my wedded life had resolved itself into a subject for detectives; the husband, whom a few months back I had sworn at the altar to love and honor and obey, had become a suspect, whose conduct must be investigated; the promise of wedded felicity had degenerated into the certainty of—a case.

I might desist even now in my attempt to understand my situation. If I did so I could live comfortably, even luxuriously to the end of my days. I was rich, and could consequently make as many friends as I chose; I was intelligent—passably so—and could interest myself in the current events of the day. I was young—ah! that was it. Why was I young? Alas! I needed love, sympathy and respect. I was womanly in spite of my eccentricities, which were those of an ignorant, obstinate girl. What woman, young and impulsive, would consent to accept a situation such as that which had been thrust upon me—or into which I had voluntarily stepped, if you will,—for I do not attempt to defend myself?

No, I would not suffer such humiliation. "Let this be the last of my scruples," I said to myself as I dressed for dinner. "Let me know exactly what stands between me and my husband's love. It may possibly be removed, and then—." I loved Arthur desperately. If I could only have hated him, how much better would it have been for me—and for him.

"Madame is feverish," said Marie, suddenly, as she watched me in my efforts to beautify myself with those fine feathers which are correctly supposed to make fine birds.

Her words gave me a shock. I looked in the glass. Yes, I was feverish. My cheeks were burning. There was a hectic red upon each. Evidently I had not succeeded in schooling myself into composure.

"What can I do, Marie?" I asked helplessly. "I do not want to have red cheeks."

Marie looked rather surprised, but her French experience thus appealed to, did me excellent service. At the end of ten minutes the color of my countenance was beautifully normal. The hectic spots had disappeared, at least from sight.

I went down to the dining-room to eat my hateful dinner with Arthur. He was in a hopelessly conventional good humor. I succeeded—admirably, I thought—in emulating his complacence. To show the effect of my determination to keep from my husband any suspicion of my thoughts and actions, I chatted pleasantly upon a variety of subjects—the hackneyed aggressiveness of Lord Randolph Churchill;[1] the new comic opera at the Savoy; the coming concert at St. James' Hall; Lady Toadyby's costume at the Queen's drawing-room; the accounts of Sardou's new play in Paris, with Bernhardt in the title role and—yes! I did it—the latest divorce case, minus the details, of course.

I read everything, understood nearly all that I read, focussed it in my mind, and you see was prepared to present it in good evening dress as an accessory to the dinner of my lord and master. I consider I did

---

1   Lord Randolph Henry Spencer-Churchill (1849-1895), British Conservative politician and Leader of the House of Commons.

bravely. I had never done better. Arthur looked up thoroughly pleased. He little knew that beneath my coat—the coat that Marie put upon my cheeks—two scarlet spots were burning, and that my soul sickened of Lord Randolph Churchill, the Savoy Theatre, St. James' Hall, Lady Toadyby and all the rest of it.

Dinner was over—thank goodness!

"Are you going out to-night, Arthur?" I asked carelessly.

"Yes, Elsie, I—I—think so. Why?"

I had long ceased to interest myself in his actions as far as he could see. He had, therefore, a right to feel rather surprised when I questioned him on the subject now.

"Nothing," I answered vaguely.

"Can I do anything for you?"

"Oh, no, thank you." I was so amiable that he was more taken aback. "I must be careful," I said to myself.

As I vouchsafed no further remark, he left me, and half an hour afterwards I heard the front door close behind him.

Now, then, if I could only aid Detective Rickaby in any way. I had several long hours before me, with nothing more inviting than a novel which had been recommended to me by dear Miss Euphemia Dasy, and which I knew I should hate, with which to distract myself.

I went at once to Arthur's study, at least as far as the door, which I found locked. I shook it rather severely, in the silly hope that it would yield to such inducements. The chivalrous and interesting James happened to pass me at the time. He cast a look of intense surprise in my direction.

"You can't get in," he said with a grin.

"So I perceive," I remarked with affected resignation, walking slowly away as James departed for the lower regions. I slipped on a big straw hat, ran into the garden, and surveyed the prospect of effecting an entrance into my husband's sanctum from that point. It was not so hopeless. The room had a large window, not more than three feet from the ground, opening into the garden. The window was shrouded with thick curtains, so that it was impossible to see from the garden into the room.

With supreme satisfaction I noticed that the window was unlocked. My course was not left long undecided. It may not have been a particularly ladylike, but it was a vigorous one. I sprang upon the window sill, stood up, and very soon saw the glass obstacle raised sufficiently to permit my entrance into the apartment.

Arthur's sanctum was a rather large room, divided by heavy plush portières[1] into two. That in which I now stood was fitted up comfortably as a writing room. There was an oak desk; one of those delightful leather-cushioned reading chairs which adjust themselves so amiably to the various positions of the most exacting body; a teeming book-case, a music canterbury[2] filled with music, and other useful articles of furniture. There were some charming pictures upon the wall and, in a word, the apartment was evidently that of a man of refinement. Bitterly, I acknowledged that fact to myself, and thus began a little logical process of reasoning which rendered me all the more miserable. Arthur was a man of refinement—he must be; there could be no use denying it; he appreciated what was refined, and despised the vulgar and the common—his room showed that. He did not appreciate me—therefore I could not be refined; he despised me—therefore I was vulgar and common. The fallacy of this reasoning is of course very evident, but it was not evident to me at that time. Can you wonder at it?

I had sunk into this reading chair, and was evidently forgetting the real object of my intrusion. I had not come here to meditate. Heaven knows, I had ample time and opportunities for that pastime elsewhere.

I pushed back the plush portières, and stood in the back portion of Arthur's sanctum. It was fitted up as a bedroom. There was a large brass bedstead a wash-stand, closets for clothes. So, when my husband did not spend the night out—and I had imagined he always did so—this was where he slept. It was rather a curious notion—but I had come to the conclusion that Arthur was rather a curious man. I wondered why he had objected to my visiting his sanctum. Surely he must have been aware that I would have preferred knowing he was in the house than supposing him out of it. Then a number of odious ideas came rushing into my head to bewilder me with the hideous probability that they were facts.

Could I discover no evidence against him without the aid of detectives? I went into the first half of the room, and tried the oak desk. The keys were in it—thank goodness! My lord had evidently grown

---

1   Door-curtains.

2   A piece of furniture with partitions for music portfolios.

careless, in the belief that he had an obedient little fool of a wife who would never dare to disobey his slightest behest. Ah! he made a mistake. I remembered my wedding day, and my mild, dutiful pleading to be allowed to inspect my husband's rooms. "They are in great disorder, Elsie," he had said. "You had better not venture into them." And my laughing rejoinder had been, "I believe you're a Bluebeard, Arthur, and that the bodies of a dozen preceding Mrs. Ravener's lie festering in that room." I opened the oak desk. It was filled with neatly arranged papers. I examined them all carefully. Alas; they were fearfully uninteresting. Old letters from his parents—I did not read them; literary efforts with the "returned with thanks," marked in tell-tale prominence; bills paid and unpaid, and similar documents of an equally useless description, as far as I was concerned. I went through them all with trembling fingers, dreading and hoping to find some incriminating papers. I was just about to leave the desk, when it suddenly occurred to me that I had missed opening one of the little drawers. I returned to my task, opened the drawer, and came across a little file of receipted bills. I had discovered so many already that I saw no use in examining them. Something prompted me however to glance at them.

They were monthly rent receipts. I read: "Received from Mr. Arthur Ravener the sum of twelve pounds for one month's rent in advance, for the furnished house, No. 121 Lancaster Road, Notting Hill, London, W., due 1st inst. Received payment, B. J. Smith."

How could that interest me? Arthur had probably lived in Lancaster Road, Notting Hill, at one period of his existence. I saw no reason why he should not have done so.

My eyes fell upon the date of the uppermost receipt. The papers dropped from my hands. I started back in terror.

The last twelve pounds acknowledged by Mr. B. J. Smith had been paid for the use of No. 121 Lancaster Road, during this month—this very month of May. Arthur had a perfect right to those premises at the present moment. He might be there now.

Oh! I saw it all now clearly before me. Tavistock Villa was the home of Arthur's neglected, despised wife; No. 121 Lancaster Road, Notting Hill, was the abode of his mistress. He loved her so well, that he could sacrifice his reputation for her. Perhaps he brought her occasionally to the room in which I now stood. To no other part of the house did he dare to take her. Over Tavistock Villa his hated wife reigned; her supremacy must not be called into question. Even then I felt a spasm of pity for Arthur. He was kind to me after all. He consulted my wishes, he gratified them, he was good and brotherly. And how difficult such a course of action must have been to him, when he daily and hourly had the image of a dearly beloved one in his mind. I loved Arthur dearly; I could not have shown the amount of endurance to another man that Arthur manifested to me. As I said, I felt a spasm of pity for Arthur. The spasm was soon over, and in its place a fury of bitterness swept over me. Who was the wretch who could take a husband so shamelessly from his wife? How did she dare to do such a thing? Had she so little knowledge of her own sex as to suppose that she would remain undiscovered very long? Did she not dread that discovery, or tremble at the inevitable meeting with an insulted and indignant wife?

I suddenly remembered where I was—in his room, and possibly in hers. I made haste to leave it. I was anxious to start for Notting Hill that moment, while the fever of animosity was burning so fiercely within me.

The cool night air calmed me somewhat. I reflected upon the inadvisability of such a hasty course. I had put my case in the hands of an able detective. I had better wait at least until I heard from him. He had asked me to try and discover any letters or papers in my husband's possession, that would lead me to the belief that I had a rival. I had been successful, I thought. Mr. Rickaby had promised to let me know where my husband went each night. I would wait until I heard from him.

I did not have to wait long. Two days later a gentleman called to see me. He would not disclose his business to James. He must see Mrs. Ravener. It was a special agent of Mr. Rickaby's private detective bureau. He had come to inform me that he had tracked my husband for two nights to—I almost laughed as he gave the address—No. 121 Lancaster Road, Notting Hill, W.

"I will go there myself," I said mentally, "I will see him in the house. I will see her—and then—" well, subsequent events should take care of themselves.

CHAPTER 17

IT was a dark, dismal sort of an evening. A small provoking rain was falling, the trees dripped incessantly, and the mud in the Kew thoroughfares was horribly and consistently thick. I sat at the window of Tavistock Villa, watching the men returning from the city to their quiet, suburban homes. I wondered if they were glad to free themselves from the much maligned atmosphere of London for this invigorating air, or if they would have preferred the metropolis, with all its unhealthy faults, to the sedate and monotonous wholesomeness of Kew.

I would sooner live ten years in the city than fifty years in the country. I hate the balmy atmosphere of rurality; I loathe the suburban surroundings. Give me the city with its life, its motion, its meaning, its excitement. I could not sympathize with rural man.

"Fixed like a plant on his peculiar spot,
To draw nutrition, propagate—and rot."[1]

---

1   Alexander Pope (1688-1744), *An Essay on Man*, Epistle 2 (63-64).

We had just dined. In a few moments I should doubtless see my husband set out for the city, and I had made up my mind that after having given him a good hour's start, I would follow him. I had matured no plans. The only thing I had decided upon doing was gaining admittance to No. 121 Lancaster Road, and then suddenly confronting the guilty couple. I would not permit any one to announce me. If Arthur in his unhallowed household kept servants, I would dispense with their aid. I would confound my husband and his paramour; I would glory in his trembling confusion, and gloat over the irremediable, hopeless guilt in which I had surprised him.

I was a jealous woman, goaded to action. There is nothing more dangerous in the animal kingdom.

I did not have to wait long for my husband's departure. I saw him hurry out into the wet, uncomfortable night, with a protecting umbrella above his head. He had merely uttered a conventional "good-night" to me, when he left the dining room. I believe he now imagined that I had settled down into the placid daily enactment of the role of an injured wife. I had fretted at first, protested, even rebelled, but now it was all over; the uselessness of such revolt had become apparent. I am convinced that those were his ideas.

I rang the bell for Marie, "Bring me my long cloak, hat and veil," I ordered; "I am going up to London at once."

"At once!" echoed Marie in surprise, "this wet night?"

"Yes," I replied impatiently, "if any one should call, you can say I have gone—Oh, anywhere."

"To Madame, your mother—to Grosvenor Square?"

"Exactly," I replied, happily untruthful. No one would call, but it was best to be on the safe side.

I covered my face with a dark veil, the hackneyed device of the mysterious woman. I did this because I was afraid I might be recognized on my way to London. I did not want tongues to wag, at least until I gave them an unqualified right to do so. I was dressed long before it was advisable to start, and threw myself into an arm-chair in the drawing-room, waiting for the minutes to pass. I was wonderfully calm, and rejoiced at that fact. Angry people generally get the worst of it in this world. Quiet wrath does more effective work than an ebullition of fury.

Half an hour later I was in the damp night air, ploughing my way through the mud. I had decided that I would go to Notting Hill by the democratic Underground Railway. So I walked as quickly as I could to the Kew station, which was not far from Tavistock Villa. I had not very long to wait for the arrival of the train. It soon came roaring into the station. I ensconced myself comfortably in a first-class carriage, and threw myself lazily back in its blue cushioned seat.

I was not alone. Two young men sat opposite to me, and to my dismay I recognized Archie Lucknow and Melville Potterby, two detestable society whipper-snappers, whose hideous mission on earth, it seemed to me, was to persecute the gentler sex with attention. Thank goodness they did not recognize me through my veil. I had no particular anxiety to be seen on the road to London at eight o'clock at night, and alone.

"I can't help thinking, dear boy," Mr. Lucknow was saying in a low tone, "how deucedly uncharitable you are. Now you brand young Honeyworth with a mark of Cain, in sheer willfulness. You have no evidence to substantiate what you say. It is cruel, positively it is, my dear boy. I am not a very straight-laced fellow, as you know, Potterby, but hang it all, if I care to hear this kind of thing."

"It is true, nevertheless," said Mr. Potterby, imperturbably. "No evidence is necessary. Eyes are evidence in this case."

"Well, we will drop the subject. You see how mistaken you were in the case of Arthur Ravener. You had branded him—everybody had, in fact. His name was on the lips of all fellows. He was shunned. What happened? He married; tongues ceased wagging, and now there is not a fellow in the crowd that maligned him, who would not be glad to apologize for his brutality."

Mr. Lucknow came to a pause. Oh! if they would continue talking! If they could only imagine how vitally interesting to me their conversation was! Perhaps it was just as well they could not imagine this, however.

"I would not apologize to Arthur Ravener," said Mr. Potterby in the same low tones, which, however, were distinctly audible to me.

"Then you are not the fellow I thought you"—very severely.

"Sorry, my dear boy, but can't help it. Before I apologize to Ravener, I'd like to know Mrs. Ravener's side of the story. People may have ceased talking. Ravener's marriage was always, in my opinion, brought about solely with that object in view. And he married a very young girl, as ignorant as a new-born babe."

"She was a silly little fool," said Mr. Lucknow, rather savagely.

I had snubbed him with great persistency, so I could not complain at his vehemence.

"Yes, and you know—" What Mr. Lucknow knew I could not learn, as Mr. Potterby's voice sank into a whisper which was hopelessly beyond my scope. They said no more. What I had heard simply whetted the edge of my curiosity. I wondered what Arthur had done, before I knew him, to cause gossip. It seemed to me that a quiet, refined young man, such as I previously supposed him to be, could not have given any very serious offence.

Perhaps, however, it was this very *liaison*, which I was now bent upon breaking, that had set his friends talking. That must be it. This horrible woman had been his bane. People had discovered her existence, and of course no young man in this enlightened century would recognize Arthur's unsavory life. I supposed that although the youths of to-day were silly and tedious they were at least strictly moral.

"Notting Hill."

Here I was at my destination. I alighted hurriedly, not daring to look at my fellow travelers, and was soon in the street. Now for No. 121 Lancaster Road.

I had no idea where it was, but a kindly policeman informed me that it was not more than seven minutes' walk from the station. He spoke the truth. Lancaster Road was so easy to find that even I could make no mistake about it.

When I had reached the thoroughfare, and commenced my search for No. 121, all the semi-jauntiness which I had called to my assistance, left me. The thought of my mission, and indignation at the causes of it, filled my mind. I began to dread my task.

Lancaster Road seemed to be deserted at this early hour. It was only nine o'clock. Not a solitary person had I passed yet. The big grey houses towered gloomily on each side of me. Bright lights shone from the windows, probably illuminating those happy homes which are in no city more plentiful than in London.

I was counting the numbers, my heart palpitating as I slowly approached that at which I should stop. I felt half inclined to go back at this eleventh hour, and live as I had been living these past few months, contentedly. No! content was no longer possible for me. I could not meet my husband again until I had seen my rival; and until he knew that I had seen her.

I stopped in front of a small gray house involuntarily. I seemed to feel instinctively, even before I had looked, that it was No. 121, and I was right. There were the three figures that to me made so sinister a combination, engraved on a little brass plate on the door. Then I took a leisurely view of the house in which Arthur chose to live, apart from his wife. It was a little, two-story, gray-stone house, old fashioned, and rather unusual in its appearance. There was a tiny green grass plot in front, separated from the road by an iron railing, in which was a small, unlatched gate. It would have been a very ordinary-looking house in a provincial city, but it was not at all suggestive of London. I looked at it with genuine curiosity, which for a moment swallowed up my anger. It was a very inexpensive place, but, love—guilty and illegitimate, but still love—dwelt there. Arthur preferred that simple little house, with one to whom he could give his heart, than the costly beauty of Tavistock Villa, with the wife whom he despised.

I brushed away the tears that rose unbidden to my eyes, with angry hands. This was no place for sentimental regret. I was here to act, and act I would.

There seemed to be only one room in the house which was lighted, and that was situated to the left of the front door. A light, reddened by warm, thick curtains, shone from its windows. Darkness reigned everywhere else. There was no light even in the hall. The glass above the front door looked black.

How was I to gain admittance? If I rang the rusty-looking front door bell it would probably alarm them both. They were doubtless prepared in case of surprise of that kind, and such a course would certainly place me at a disadvantage. It was not likely that they kept servants, who might in the future prove unfortunate witnesses against them.

What could I do? I pushed open the gate and walked towards the stone steps leading to the front door. A thin iron grating separated me from the basement entrance. I touched it, and I could feel the gritty rust on my fingers. This basement entrance was in all likelihood never used now. I shook the grating slightly. Imagine my surprise, my joy, when it yielded without any difficulty to my gentle persuasion, and stood open.

I entered immediately, only too pleased to be shut out from the sight of any passerby, or of any policeman, to whom my position would have appeared rather strange.

I shut the iron gate behind me, descended two steps, and walked into the kitchen. It was in utter darkness. Not an object in front of me could I see. I groped my way about, feeling distinctly uneasy. Whether this kitchen were ever used, or whether it were in ruins I could not tell. I would have given a sovereign for a match—for one moment's light.

I presumed that this house was built like most houses, so I did not despair of finding my way upstairs. I could not discover the door leading to the basement hall, nor that by which I had entered. I grew frightened. The awful idea dawned upon me that I might have to stay where I was until daylight. I almost shrieked as I stumbled against some resisting object. It was nothing more alarming than a chair. I sat down and tried to quiet myself. My heart was throbbing wildly, and I could feel violent pulsations in my temples. They might hear me upstairs. The noise I made might alarm them. They would leave the house. I should be its sole tenant, and—

I started up. I would not terrify myself by such thoughts. By a mighty effort I collected myself as it were, and began my ridiculous hunt for the door with more deliberation. I was rewarded by success.

I had gained the stairs. I walked slowly upwards, found the door at the top of the stairs open—what should I have done had it been locked?—and stood in the hall. Now I could see the door of the room for which I was bound. The hall was in absolute darkness, but faint streaks of light, which would have been unnoticed under less obscure circumstances, revealed to me the whereabouts of the guilty couple. It was impossible now that they could escape me. I must see them. As this certainty forced itself upon me, my excitement became all the more intense.

I did not dare to move. From behind the hall door where I had retreated, I surveyed the situation. Six or eight steps would take me to the room where I could discover all. The door would in all probability be unlocked. From whom had they to fear intrusion? They were safely secluded—or they fancied they were—in their own castle. I had only to suddenly open the door and face them.

My courage began to fail me. My position was an unenviable one. I wondered how matters would be three hours from now—if everything would be settled; if I should have discovered all. Then I carefully lacerated my feelings by reviewing events connected with my unhappy marriage. I pictured my absurd scruples. I had heard that evening that I was a silly little fool. That was the truth. I was silly, I was unworthy—

Without concluding my self-condemnation, I rushed from my hiding-place to the door of the room whence came the light. Without hesitating one moment I turned the handle, and giving a mighty push, which was absolutely unnecessary, I entered.

The sudden light coming upon my eyes, accustomed for the last half hour to utter darkness, blinded me. I could see nothing. Then two figures abruptly moving stood out before me in the glare. My dazzled inability lasted but a few seconds. Then before me I saw my husband, pale as death, trembling, his eyes wide with amazement, advancing towards me. I waved him off, standing with my back to the door. The room was a small one. At the other end of it was his companion.

The amazement of Arthur was not as great as that which must have been visible on my own face, as I beheld, ghastly in his pallor, but still boldly defiant—Captain Jack Dillington.

I burst into hysterical laughter.

CHAPTER 18

CAPTAIN Dillington and my husband seemed unable to utter a word. My laughter did not last long. Quick as a flash of lightning came the thought to me that I was in a very ridiculous situation. After having shown my hand in a most hopeless manner, I had discovered my husband *tête-à-tête* with—the abandoned woman I had pictured, the wanton destroyer of my domestic happiness I had imagined? No, with his bosom friend—the friend who long before I had come upon the scene had played the role of Damon to Arthur's Pythias.

Of course, as I stood before them, my hysterical laughter silenced, my breast heaving with emotion, and the fever spot burning on each cheek, they knew why I was there, what I suspected. But was it merely my sudden arrival that was responsible for the death-like pallor of my husband's face? Why did Captain Dillington assume such a palpably defiant air, if there were no reason why he should defy me?

Such thoughts coursed through my mind much quicker than they can flow from my pen. After all had I shown my hand? Yes and no. I remembered that my mother had suggested Captain Dillington as the medium by which my husband communicated with his paramour. Why not assume that, in default of anything more substantial? That Captain

Dillington was in some way responsible for my husband's despicable conduct, I was now as convinced as that I saw him before me. He had some influence over Arthur Ravener, the weaker vessel. This idea gained complete supremacy over me. It was then with Captain Dillington that I would deal—this deadly friend whom I would hold responsible.

I stood before the door, as I said, and simply stared at the two men, after my laughter had been subdued. Arthur grasped the back of a chair, and stood looking at me, as though he were obliged to look. Captain Dillington took a seat with a mighty show of composure, and awaited developments.

Arthur was the first to speak, and he did so gaspingly, "Why—why—d-did you c-come here, Elsie?" he asked.

"Why—why—did I come here?" I repeated mockingly.

"It is quite natural that your wife should be here, Arthur," said the Captain in his most elaborate manner. "She had suspicions—most natural, my dear fellow. She was jealous. You have no right to complain. Jealousy, as I look upon it, is merely an outcome of love. Is that not so, Mrs. Ravener?" (turning to me) "You—pardon my curiosity—thought that you would find a—a—well—a lady with your husband?"

The leer with which he accompanied these remarks was too indescribably repulsive to analyze. I determined to contain myself as much as possible.

"It is with no lady that I have business here," I said, with a miserable attempt at loftiness. "It is with you, Captain Dillington, and with no other."

I watched the effect of these words, shot at random. It was undeniable. Captain Dillington gasped. The blood left his cheeks and his lips. He was taken utterly aback. I had evidently started in the right direction. He must be the go-between, but as I had seen no woman, it was not necessary that I should mention one.

"You are surprised, Captain Dillington?" I demanded quietly, though I was trembling with agitation.

"I—I simply do not understand you."

"Do you understand me, Arthur?" I asked, turning to my husband.

"I—I will not listen to your suspicions," began my husband, with such a weak attempt at resistance that it sounded more like an entreaty.

"Elsie, you have no right here. You—you betray w-want of confidence in—in me. I will not stay—"

"You will!" I cried, placing my back to the door. "You shall not leave this room. Don't dare to try it," I continued, losing all my calmness, as a tide of anger swept over me, overwhelming caution. "Captain Dillington, if you attempt to stir from the room" (he had made a step forward) "I will open the window and rouse the neighbors. I don't mind scandal, perhaps, as much as you and he do. I can explain my presence here. You cannot."

"This is your husband's house," said, Captain Dillington, angrily. "He has invited me here. I have nothing to explain. While I was a guest at your house, it was easy to see that I was not welcome. Your husband saw it. I saw it. So as we have always been great friends, he chose to invite me where there was no danger of my being insulted. That explains my presence here, I think."

"No, it does not. That does not explain your presence here, and you know it. You know it too, Arthur Ravener," I cried, turning to the helplessly distressed object all in a heap on the back of a chair. "Do you think, Captain Dillington, that I will continue to tolerate the conduct of this man, who left me on my wedding day, and who kept you a hated guest—yes, you are right, a hated, detested, loathed guest—in our house, when it should have been sacred to ourselves? Do you think that because I am young and ignorant—no, I am no longer ignorant—that I will bear with this? You know very little of women if you can suppose it. You probably thought you were dealing with a helpless fool. Let me tell you that you have been watched by detectives for the past week, at my instigation, and that I know all."

It was a desperate game of bluff, but it met with triumphant success. As I paused for want of breath, I saw that Captain Dillington was literally unable to speak.

He had warmed himself into anger a few moments before, but in the shock of this great surprise, it had died away. My husband had averted his face, and was looking at the wall with very great persistence. So far the field was my own. I had worked myself into a great passion, and these hits had not been premeditated.

"I will live no longer as I have been doing," I went on, "I have discovered enough. I have hoped against hope. I have dreaded this hour.

But it has come, and I will not fear it. I have told you that I do not mind scandal, and I shall not hesitate to apply to the Divorce Court."

Captain Dillington pressed his hand to his heart. My husband came towards me, and took my hand.

"Elsie," he said, "do not—do not, for the love of Heaven speak like this. You cannot mean what you say. You cannot, you would not do it?"

"I would," I exclaimed, furiously, "I would do it. You have tried my patience. I have no interest in you any more. I gave you all, and you have treated me with contempt. I will not live with you any longer. I will not—I could not. The thought of your infamy would rise up before me at all times. I will be free, and you shall, you must be free, too."

I burst into tears, I could not help it. After all, I had done bravely, and I was not made of stone. I had ceased to wonder who was the woman in the case. I had succeeded in confounding the two men so well without her aid, that I felt comparatively satisfied. In fact I did not want to know who she was.

Captain Dillington recovered himself somewhat when he saw my tears. "Mrs. Ravener forgets that in a divorce suit a great many things must be proved. You say you have had us watched by detectives. May I ask if they have discovered the identity of the co-respondent?"

The coolness with which he spoke almost amused me. I laughed amidst my sobs. "I—I have all the evidence I need," I managed to say. "Suppose," with an attempt at mirth, "I—I should make you co-respondent, Captain Diliington?"

He smiled, but it was with a great effort, I could see.

"Very good, very good," he said, with manifest uneasiness.

"Do not—do not talk like that, Elsie," said Arthur, imploringly. "You will not bring this—this scandal upon us all. You—you did love me, Elsie. I do not believe that I have quite killed your love. You would not ruin me like this. You would not bring disgrace upon your family." He broke down, sobbing.

"The disgrace," I said sternly, feeling contempt for these pitiful arguments, "is brought by you, sir. My character is spotless, as you well know. I have given you every opportunity to avoid scandal, but you failed to suppose that I could do anything but submit to your heartless neglect. You have aroused me. It has taken you twelve months to do it. If you had married a girl who had mixed more with the world, she would not have lived with you one week. I had peculiarities, however, and you thought they would give you an opportunity to carry out your wretched plans without interruption; that is why you married me. I was warned against you—you need not start—but I disregarded the warning, and I have dearly paid for my folly. My punishment has been great, but it shall end from to-day. To-morrow I will leave Tavistock Villa, and I never want to see it again."

I began to button my cloak and gloves. I had said enough. I would now leave them to do exactly what they chose. I had no more interest in my husband, I told myself.

"You are going, Mrs. Ravener?" queried Captain Dillington in a mocking tone, his jeering exuberance once more asserting itself.

"I am going," I said.

Arthur seized his hat, and sprang towards the door. "I will go with you, Elsie," he said in a pleading tone.

"You will not," I exclaimed. "You shall not enter the house—with me, at any rate."

"He has a perfect right to do so," remarked Captain Dillington. "It is his home; you are his wife."

"And you—?" I asked pointedly. My jest about the co-respondent in the case had annoyed him so much before, that I thought I would administer another stab with the same weapon.

He turned away hastily for a moment. "I am his friend," he then said, "and"—boldly—"I am not ashamed of it. We were at college together, and our intimacy has been continued since those days. I will aid Arthur Ravener whenever I can; I will do anything for him. He is my bosom friend, and I am ready to say so before anybody. Now, are you satisfied?"

He snapped his fingers defiantly, but I was not going to allow myself to be beaten. My game of bluff had been successful. Perhaps he was trying the same tactics. He should not succeed.

"As far as you are concerned—perfectly," I said.

I opened the door. Arthur followed me.

"If you persist in coming," I said, "of course you must do so. After all, it does not make much difference; your apartments do not clash with mine."

He winced, but said nothing. He cast a glance, uneasy, suspicious, wretched, at Captain Dillington, and then left the room with me. He opened the front door, and we stepped out into the night air. Captain

Dillington remained where we left him. Not another word did he utter.

"Shall I call a cab?" asked Arthur, nervously.

"If you choose," I said carelessly. "You insist upon accompanying me, so that I cannot help myself. Oblige me, however, by not troubling to talk. I have nothing to say. I don't want any explanation. That house," pointing to No. 121 Lancaster Road, "speaks for itself."

He hailed a passing four-wheeler, and we were soon rolling homewards. I buried my face in the cushions, and resolutely declined to think of my grievance during the long, weary ride home. Arthur made no attempt to speak. He stared, in a dazed way, out of the side windows, though he could not have seen much; and so we reached Tavistock Villa.

CHAPTER 19

THERE is one malady dear to the heart of modern novel-writers. It is helpful, pleasantly dangerous, and yet to be vanquished. Of course I allude to brain fever. Once get your hero into some scrape from which there is no outlet, and you are forced to call upon brain fever for help. He lies dangerously ill for weeks, months; makes several delirious confessions; arises once more the ghost of his former self, and in the meantime, what? All difficulties have been smoothed away, and the eager interest of the unsuspecting reader has been relieved of its keen edge. Brain fever is a boon to the novel-writer, and like all cheap boons it has been woefully abused.

Brain fever, however, is not nearly as frequent in real life as it is in novels. It is fiction's way out of a climax.

I have jotted down these thoughts because I remember they occurred to me during the days which followed the events described in the preceding chapter, when time hung heavily on my hands, and I could settle to nothing.

When we reached Tavistock Villa on that important night, Arthur retired to the rooms he had fitted up for himself, and I went silently to my own apartments. We attempted no explanations. We had no word to say. There was not even an uttered "good-night."

Next morning my husband sent for me, and I went at once to his room. He told me he had not slept all night, except for a few minutes at a time, when he had been awakened by alarming dreams. His face was flushed and his eyes moved constantly. It was easy to see that he was ill.

"Elsie," he said, "if people should call to-day, t-tell them that I—I am indisposed—th-that I cannot see them. You will do this?"

"No one shall disturb you," I promised. "We will have a doctor, presently, for I am afraid you are indeed indisposed."

"Do not send for a doctor," he said, excitedly, "I do not need one. I do not, indeed, Elsie, I assure you."

"You are mistaken," I said, coldly. "I insist upon sending for Dr. White. Perhaps you will allow me to have my own way for once."

He looked at me reproachfully. I felt guilty—as though I were hitting a man when he was down. Dr. White came. He said that Arthur must have been subjected to some long-continued mental anxiety, and that he needed careful nursing. I was not to be unnecessarily alarmed if at times he had hallucinations, such as imagining himself surrounded by enemies, or suspecting that people were plotting to do him harm. His nervous system was run down.

"Your husband has not been living as quietly as he might have done, I infer, Mrs. Ravener?" Dr. White asked rather hesitatingly.

I crimsoned. How could I tell this man that my husband's pursuits were unknown to me? He noticed my confusion.

"Dr. White," I said at last, deliberately, resolved to tell as much as I could, "I see no use in concealment. A medical man must receive strange confidences. The truth is that I know little more about my husband's life than you do. All I can tell you is that during the last year he has spent most of his time out of the house."

"Exactly," with significance. "I thought as much," with sapient consideration; then, "Well, Mrs. Ravener, if you will take my advice, you will forgive everything, and make no allusion whatever to the past. What your husband needs is complete rest and change, and a few months' devotion to him on your part will restore him to you. My dear young lady, this is not an unusual case—"

I started up. "Not unusual?" I interrupted. Then I reflected that all he knew of the case, and all that I intended he should know, might not be unusual.

"Not unusual," he said. "Young men of fortune like your husband, marrying at an early age, cannot break suddenly from old associations, from bachelor friends, from—ah! how do I know? That is why I always say to friends who I hear are about to wed: 'Reflect well, my boy. A wife is exacting. She will call you to account for yourself. All your gay doings must be renounced. A woman gives herself up to you. You must reciprocate.' You love your husband?" he asked, suddenly jerking his voice from an anecdotal crooning to a professional tone.

"Yes," I said in a low voice.

"Then, Mrs. Ravener, it is a case of plain sailing. Try to forget your injuries. Leave this country as soon as you conveniently can, and take your husband with you. What would you think of a trip across the Atlantic to America? It would be the making of you both. If," stammering, "as y-you suspect, and—as—I—suspect, Mr. Ravener—er—has—er—ties—er—here, which he should not have—er—what better means of breaking them could you possibly discover?"

He was right, the scheme was an excellent one. All this time I had been giving way to my indignant anger at my husband's cruel treatment, but I had never thought of attempting to remove him from temptation. Here was I planning separation, divorce and other scandalously revengeful proceedings, when, in reality, perhaps all my husband wanted was a change. He was weak, and he was under the influence of a man with an iron will, I felt sure. Perhaps I might be a little too submissive, but Arthur was my husband and I loved him.

"Dr. White," I said, rising and taking the old man's hand, "I—I thank you, your suggestion is a kind one—so kind and good that—that—it would not have occurred to me."

I buried my face in my hands. Yes, I was too vindictive. Even this morning, when I had seen Arthur feverish and oppressed, I could not forget the past few months. I thought only of my own wrongs. Who knew but that Arthur was as much sinned against as sinning? In this world too much charity is impossible.

"Mrs. Ravener," said Dr. White, pretending not to see my tears, "I have left a prescription on the little table in your husband's room. See that it is made up. I will look in again. You have nothing to be alarmed about. Your husband will recover, and—my dear—I hope that you will both, like the good people in the fairy tales, live happily ever after. Now, now—no tears," he said, placing his hand on my bowed head. "Be as cheerful as you possibly can. I always say that my prescriptions should be diluted with cheerfulness. Ah! it is a wonderful thing."

While he was talking, I rose and dried my eyes. By the time he had finished, I could smile at him. He was satisfied and left me. As he went from the room, James entered with a card. "The gentleman is waiting," he said, with a quick look in my face.

The card was that of Captain Dillington. I tore it up savagely, forgetful of the servant's presence, and flung the pieces into the empty fireplace.

"Tell Captain Dillington," I said, "that Mr. Ravener is ill this morning and cannot be seen. If he calls again, tell him the same thing. James," approaching him, "do me a favor—it will indeed be a great one. Never permit Captain Dillington to set his foot within this house again. You will do this?"

"Yes, ma'am," he said, pleased at being asked to confer a favor, "I will. The Captain tried to brush past me this morning, but I heard the master tell you not to let people see him. I was in the room at the time, you know. So I just pushed the Captain back. He gives me a terrible look, but looks don't hurt any one. 'I'll take your card,' says I, and when he sees that I mean it he hands me one."

"You have done well," I said.

I was determined that Captain Dillington should see Arthur no more. Exactly what was the understanding between them, I did not know, but that the elder man was partly accountable for the delinquencies of the younger, I was perfectly persuaded. At any rate I would be on the safe side. I would refuse Captain Dillington admittance every time he applied for it, without consulting Arthur.

During the next few days I was constantly in my husband's room. As Dr. White led me to expect, he had hallucinations. He seemed to fancy that someone was pursuing him, but it was impossible to shape his incoherent utterances into any intelligible form. They lasted but for a short time, and left him weak, but entirely rational.

"Arthur," I said on one of these occasions, "I have a proposition to make to you. We have never taken any journey together"—I was going to refer to the lacking honeymoon, but determined to avoid any allusion to the past—"and I should like to go away very much. Suppose we were to take a trip to America?" I watched his face. His eyes fell. He turned away his head.

"It is very far," he said vaguely.

"Yes," I assented cheerfully, "that is why I am so anxious to take the trip. I think a little sail on the herring-pond would do us good," I continued, with an abortive attempt to be funny. "Dr. White said you needed a change."

"When would you want to go?" he asked uneasily.

"Any time, dear" I said. Then, as if the idea had come to me suddenly, "I think it would be best to start at once. Suppose that as soon as you are able to go out, your first ride be to Liverpool?"

He was embarrassed. "I will think it over," he said weakly. He never alluded to my threats of divorce. He seemed to have forgotten all about them. Since he had been ill, I had been kind, and as much like my former self as I possibly could.

Two days passed. Arthur's health was improving rapidly. We could start now at any time he chose to name, but he seemed in no hurry to refer to our American trip.

On the third day, when I tried to enter Arthur's room, I found the door locked. I was alarmed and knocked until my knuckles complained very painfully. I stopped suddenly, arrested by a noise I heard in the room. It could only have been the opening or shutting of the window, but it sounded strangely to me. I knocked again. Arthur hastened to the door and opened it. His face was red, and he seemed agitated. I looked at him in surprise.

"Why did you lock the door?" I asked, not sharply but curiously.

"Why not?" he said with a nervous laugh, "is there any law against it, Elsie?"

"None that I know of," I said, still rather uneasy in my mind. "Were you out in the garden, Arthur?"

"I? No."

"I thought I heard the window open?"

"My dear Elsie," he said, "why should I go into the garden by the window? You forget I am not strong enough yet to jump. If I wanted a walk, I should suggest an airing in a proper way." Arthur's manner was by no means reassuring.

"Then the window was not open?" I asked carelessly.

He hesitated a moment. "No," he replied, "it was not."

The matter was certainly not worth pursuing any further. I could have sworn that I had heard the window shut, but then perhaps my imagination, stimulated by a locked door, may have led me into error.

That night Arthur informed me he would accompany me to America any time I chose. I was delighted, and thought of nothing but the probable success of our journey away from scenes fraught with so many painful associations.

CHAPTER 20

O NCE away from Kew, and my old spirits reasserted themselves. As we rolled away from Euston to Liverpool's only and original Lime Street, I was as happy as—I was going to say—a newly-made bride, but, alas, that hackneyed simile has no meaning for me. Every old corn field we passed delighted me; I made Arthur buy me illustrated papers and fruit at every station, and nearly caused him to miss the train at one halting place because in my insatiable desire for chocolate I sent him forth to the refreshment room.

Arthur was at first inclined to be subdued, as I suppose it was proper he should be, but I soon thwarted his intentions. I was determined that we would both of us forget the past, and start out afresh. I would be as engaging as a maiden yet to be wooed, and he,—well, he should woo me. I was resolved that I would not be wifely. I would consider that we were simply on good terms, and I was going to try hard to make him love me. Pshaw! A fig for the fact that I was really his wife. He would be glad to remember that by and by, I told myself.

So I broke every bit of ice I saw, and long before we had reached Lime Street, he was laughing at my idiotic behavior. We made a couple of fools of ourselves.

I wonder why English people who take railway journeys feel that they must eat as soon as the train starts. It has always caused me a great deal of amusement. On this particular occasion, a phlethoric old matron waited until she had waved her chubby hand at about fifty fond relations on the platform, allowed a tear or two to course portentously down her cheeks, and then sought consolation in her hamper. For the next thirty minutes she was busily engaged in dissecting a chicken. Ugh! how greasy she was at the end of that time. I was rude enough to stare at her, and I presume the poor old soul thought I coveted her chicken. She offered me some. At first I thought of accepting it and going halves with Arthur, but I caught his imploring glance and decided to be abstemious.

Of course we traveled with the usual ruddy-faced Briton, who before he was fifteen minutes out was caught peeping into a little spirit flask. They always amuse me—those exploring tipplers who seem anxious to impress you with the idea that they are merely making a scientific test. I have a detestation for red noses, both male and female, which of course means that I very frequently have one in cold weather—or at least used to do so, until I discovered that perfect French jewel, Marie, my maid. Dear readers, you will never know what comfort is until you have a Gallic "assistant." Of course they are expensive luxuries, but you can economize elsewhere.

My pen runs on. As I think of that delightful trip, coming as it did when life seemed darkest, all my happiness comes back to me, and I write now as I felt then.

As I was not desirous of parading myself, limp and seasick, before a select and fashionable audience, we decided not to patronize a Cunarder,[1] even though it be so rapid. I was not so burningly anxious to be in America. I did not care where I was, so rejoiced was I to be away from London. So we ensconced ourselves meekly on one of the Inman steamers, which was quite good enough for me.

It seemed unnatural, going away without anyone to see us off, especially as nearly every one on board cried farewell to somebody on the tender.[2] I felt hard-hearted because I "sailed away from my native land,"

---

1   A British shipping company, the Cunard Line operated passenger ships on the North Atlantic.

2   Supply vessel.

without a tear. I tried to be affected, but I couldn't. I wished that I had given the polite little fellow, who had carried my valise for me, half-a-crown extra to cry when the steamer started, and wave his hand to me.

"You are as bad as I am, Arthur," I said, as we stood at the rail and watched the tender taking its farewell-sayers back to the dock. "There's not a solitary tear trickling down your countenance. I'm really vexed with myself, but they won't trickle. I can't help it."

"I am glad of it, Elsie," said Arthur, fervently. I knew he was thinking that they had trickled sufficiently during the past few sad weeks.

"I am not," I persisted in declaring. "It is unseemly to go about with all one's unshed tears while everybody else is lavishly distributing them in all directions."

No sooner had the tender disappeared from sight, and our own anchor had been lifted (isn't that deliciously nautical? I flatter myself it is extremely creditable), than I saw sixteen people—I counted them—rush up to the Captain and ask him if it were going to be "rough." Poor man! I suppose he is overwhelmed in this manner at every trip.

He thought it was going to be one of the finest voyages he had ever made, he said, and the sixteen timid ones went their way rejoicing.

It is the correct thing, nowadays, to be eternally and consistently *blasé*, as my dear mother would say, especially on one's travels. To speak of my transatlantic trip of course makes it at once apparent that I have never been to America before. I admit it, and must also confess that my voyage interested me immensely, and all the more because my expected seasickness was never realized.

To have seen us all in the saloon on the first night was in itself an entertainment. We were all very stiff, and suspicious, and unfriendly, being mostly English, and took our places at the table under protest as it were. We were soon supplied with passenger lists, and before attempting to nourish our bodies we fed our curiosity by wondering "who was who," and trying to "locate" the different passengers.

There were at least a score whose identity we soon discovered. They belonged to that class which an American on board declared to be composed of "chronic kickers—gentlemen who, if they went to Heaven, would vow their halo's didn't fit." They found that their names had been spelled wrong, and complained loudly:

"I made a point of spelling S-m-y-t-h-e and here they have me down as Smith."

"I call it disgusting. They've made me John P. Bodley, when I distinctly remember telling them my name was J. Porterhouse Bodley."

"Oh, Mamma, they've never mentioned Jane. I wanted them to put 'and maid.' How annoying!"

"Why, Eliza! They've actually got us 'J. Rogers, wife and family,' in one line, instead of mentioning each of our names, as I asked them to do."

And so they made themselves known.

The first meal was the only one of which many of the passengers approved. They had made up their minds to be seasick, and seasick they were. One young woman announced that she had been under medical treatment for three days before starting, and that her doctor had advised her after the first meal to go to bed during the rest of the voyage. That such a man should be allowed to practice!

Arthur and I sat at the Captain's table, close by the Captain, which I am told was a great honor. That dignitary seemed to wish us to think so, at any rate. He was full of graceful condescension at first, and three courses had sped quickly away before he favored us with our first nautical story. Of course everyone at the table was convulsed with laughter. It put us all in a good temper, and led us to look upon one another with less suspicion.

After dinner Arthur and I walked up and down deck, talking gaily of our plans. Not a sentimental word passed from my lips; no one could have been more affectionate and sisterly than I was. I firmly believe that he understood and appreciated my efforts. He looked at me gratefully from time to time. That friendliness which had been so oppressive in his manner to me formerly, was not so apparent.

I pictured our return to England, the past forgotten like an ugly dream; the future full of promise; the present given up utterly to the love which though late might overwhelm us with its long delayed delight. As I painted the glowing probabilities on my susceptible mind-canvas, I could not school my voice to the mild, platonic utterances which I felt I must affect. Words of love rose to my lips; I trembled at my own emotion.

"Are you not glad to be—to be here?" I asked him as quietly as I could.

He paused for one moment. Then in a low tone—"Yes," he said.

He was sincere. But there was none of the passion in his voice that I—unhappy girl!—could not keep from mine. He gave me affection in return for love. Well, at any rate, he seemed to be thawing. I had every reason to rejoice.

As I said before, I was not seasick. When we arrived at Queenstown, I recognized the fact that I had slept soundly, and arose in the best of spirits. I found my husband on deck, watching the men carrying the mail-bags on board. He also had slept well, he informed me.

It was a superb day, a bright sky overhead, a lovely green opaque sea around us, while the pretty coast of Ireland, as seen from Queenstown's snug little harbor, completed a most fascinating picture. We were both of us in excellent spirits, and chatted lightly on every subject but that of ourselves. We laughed at the queer old creatures who clambered up the sides of the big ship and cajoled us into purchasing murderous looking blackthorns, bog-oak ornaments of the most funereal type, and other quaintly Hibernian wares. How charming Ireland is—from a distance!

As we left Queenstown, people seemed to have made themselves at home on board, and to have resigned themselves to something more than a week of irrevocable sea. Men who had made their first appearance clad in the height of fashion, were hardly to be known in their hideous-comfortable sea-garments. Traveling caps replaced the shining *chapeau-de-soie*;[1] loose warm ulsters, the daintily fitting overcoats; while time-honored trousers were called into a brief resurrection. The ladies donned their plainest, most unbecoming attire. Anyone who had a grudge against any particular dress, wore it. There is little coquetry in attire on shipboard. Woman, from a pictorial point of view at any rate, is at her worst. Perhaps for the first time in her life, she is caught napping, so far as her attire is concerned.

A great number of the feminine passengers installed themselves with graceful invalidism on steamer chairs rug-enveloped. They were so determined to be ill that I should really have sympathized with their disappointment had Neptune declined to affect them as they expected to be affected.

---

1   Silk hat.

We were soon one big family, united in the common desire of reaching port speedily and safely. I had so many acquaintances before a week was ended, that my days were entirely taken up with them. We had our little scandal society on board, and discussed at afternoon tea those who were not at the table. Womanhood always finds its level, and womanhood is not womanhood without gossip.

The queer things I was told about America on that ship! One portly damsel took me to one side and informed me in a mysterious whisper that clothes were terribly expensive in America, but that I could purchase undergarments for next to nothing. Another American told me that New York houses were so much more civilized than London dwellings, because they all had stoops. What a stoop was, I had no idea. After a time it occurred to me that the houses must be trying to follow the example of the leaning tower of Pisa. That stooped. I received information on all sides, and as my mind was pleasantly blank in regard to the country discovered by Christopher Columbus, I was pounced upon by everybody who wanted to talk.

My husband rarely left my side. He never entered the smoking-room, and kept distinctly aloof from the other men. We were hardly ever alone. With the exception of a half-hour's stroll on deck each evening after dinner, my husband and I never enjoyed a *solitude à deux*.[1] Those brief half hours were devoted to general conversation. We never referred to the troublous period that had preceded our voyage.

I was rather glad that my time was so much occupied by my friend-passengers. I was able to acknowledge very soon the fact that my husband found increasing pleasure in my society. Our after dinner walks, I could see, were very pleasant to him, and at the end of a week conversation grew less general.

One evening he was unusually silent, and I made no effort to talk. We sat looking at the foamy milk-path that marked the course of the ship. I soon felt that his eyes were fastened on my face. I did not speak. My policy was not to attempt to force results in any way.

"Elsie," he said, presently, "some time ago I remember saying to you that perhaps our marriage was a mistake." I started. He went on: "I now believe that it was not. Elsie, no other woman would have been as patient

---

1   Being alone together.

as you have been, or made the sacrifice you have made in—in—really expatriating yourself for my sake. I—I—am very grateful, dear."

"You have nothing to be grateful for," I said, gravely. Then lightly throwing off the sentimental mood to which I would have loved to give sway, "I don't consider this expatriation, this is merely a pleasant voyage, and it is even more delightful than I anticipated."

"It is delightful," he said, seriously.

I imagine our fellow-passengers considered that we were rather eccentric. The men seemed to look down upon Arthur—or at least I thought so. What looked to me like contemptuous glances were cast by them at my husband when he was sitting in the midst of the medley of feminine passengers, who had evidently "taken a fancy" to me. Arthur seemed indifferent to these manifestations, if he noticed them at all. But they aroused in me a feeling of violent indignation. I could have gone up to these whipper-snappers and told them that I believed my husband to be better than they were; but perhaps it was lucky I did not adopt this course.

I was quite ready and eager to forgive Arthur everything. I had resolved that not a single allusion to my unknown rival should ever cross my lips, unless, of course, my husband showed himself to be subsequently unworthy of my love, which I did not believe he would do. I had not the faintest curiosity to know who the woman was. In fact I was glad I was absolutely ignorant on the subject. As soon as I felt convinced that our happiness was assured, I had promised myself that I would try to understand the influence which Captain Dillington possessed over my husband, and then gently to withdraw him from it. It was bad. I was quite certain of that.

And so, more happily than I had imagined even in my most sanguine moments, our voyage across the Atlantic was accomplished. We said goodbye to the friends we had made on board as sorrowfully as though we had known them for a lifetime, and prepared to join the busy throng in the American metropolis.

CHAPTER 21

WE went to a quiet hotel, "on" Broadway, but far from the noise and bewildering traffic of that turbulent thoroughfare. It was a comfortable, unostentatious little house, not startlingly impressive, like some of the caravansaries miles above us, nor gloomily monotonous like the so-called family hotels where women who are too disgracefully lazy to attend to household duties, and men who are too idiotically weak-willed to protest against this, abide in stupid sloth.

We had a dainty little suite of three rooms. There was a small, prettily furnished parlor, from one side of which Arthur's room opened, while from the other side my own chamber could be entered. It was a tiny, kitchenless flat, and—as the colored handmaiden who attended to our wants, expressed it—it was "just as cute as could be."

No more complete diversion from the painful events of the past could have been desired than this visit to New York, where everything was new to us; where suggestion from associations was out of the question; where we were unlikely to meet a soul whom we knew; where even the English newspapers, when they reached us, were ten days old, and consequently uninteresting, and where no social claims could form an excuse for separation.

The programme of our first few days in America was as follows: Breakfast at ten o'clock in that dear little parlor, which, I reflected, was gradually becoming all that separated us the one from the other; a glance through the American newspapers, so that no one could accuse us of living entirely out of the world; a drive, either through that magnificent park, which does not boast what I have always wilfully considered an intolerable nuisance, a "Rotten Row," upon what New Yorkers call "the road"; then dinner in the big dining-room. After dinner we retired to our own little parlor and I read from some popular novel to my husband. I did not weary him with instructive books, because I thought he needed recreation, and because I hate instructive books myself. I recollect how I used to have Smiles' "Self-Help"[1] thrust upon me by an enterprising governess, because she said it was "the most instructive, and at the same time the most amusing book," she could find.

I read to Arthur some good modern novels. When I saw that the dose was sufficient, I desisted, quickly closed my book, kissed him, and departed into my room.

And this treatment, I flattered myself, was most efficacious. I do not believe I gave a thought to my unknown rival during all those pleasant, happy days. I am sure I should have known it if I had. I loved my husband so dearly in this voluntary exile, that I was quick to notice his every look and expression, to account for them, to understand them.

He was gratified. Slowly but surely I was able to recognize in his manner a change from the wooed to the wooer. Alas! that a woman should ever be forced to woo a man. Still, when that man is her own husband, there are extenuating circumstances to be placed to her credit, as I think you will readily agree. My attentions did not weary him. Once or twice I grew tired of reading aloud, and he noticed it before I did. Then quietly but firmly he took the book from my unwilling hands, closed it, and laid it gently on the sofa. The slight but embarrassing pause which followed that action was broken by comments he made upon the story in question, that led to an amiable discussion of its merits, its probabilities, its characters. I gave my views with my usual

---

1   *Self-Help* (1859), by Scottish writer Samuel Smiles (1812-1904), was a best-selling treatise on the importance of hard work and perseverance.

flippant recklessness, and at last had the delight of knowing that I entertained him.

I believe I have called my married life unhappy. Ah! why should I say that, with the memory of those few sunny days vividly before me? Nothing can take that memory away from me. Those days were mine; I had worked for them laboriously, and they came simply as the reward of labor. I earned them. They were not the fullest joy that could have been given me, but they were inexpressibly dear, and as I think of them my eyes moisten and my lips tremble.

At the dinner-table, one night, we heard a very spirited discussion upon the merits of a sensational preacher, who was attracting large audiences— yes, "audiences" is the correct word—to his church, and exciting a good deal of newspaper comment at the same time. The majority of those who took part in the discussion were inclined to the opinion that the reverend gentleman was far too secular in his pulpit addresses; while the minority contended that he struck bravely at the root of crying evils from the very best place where it was possible for a man to strike at them. What was a pulpit for, said they, if not to redress evils by ventilating them? They, for their part, did not care to listen to the old-fashioned sermons that pleased generations past. The sermons might not be orthodox in the accepted meaning of the word, but they were interesting, clever and virile.

"Let us go to-morrow and hear this much-talked-about gentleman, Arthur," I said to my husband as we returned to our parlor after dinner. "We can then pass upon his merits or demerits in our own particularly learned way. What say you?"

He laughed.

"We will go, Elsie," he said. "You shall pass upon his merits or demerits as usual, and I will simply curb your impetuosity in whatever direction you may argue—also, as usual."

So the following morning, which happened to be Sunday, instead of casting our eyes through the voluminous newspapers, we disposed ourselves to thoughts of church, a novelty to both of us, I am sorry, though obliged, to confess.

This home of sensationalism was a very modern-looking building— as, of course, was appropriate. I was surprised when I found that it was a church, so extremely secular was its appearance.

It was situated a long way from our hotel, but in what street I cannot remember, though I am quite sure it was above Fortieth Street and below Fiftieth.

Crowds of people were entering the building as we reached it—exquisitely dressed women, black-clad respectable-looking men, and comely children in all their Sunday finery. I was told that this was a distinctly American congregation. It was certainly a most refined and intelligent-looking gathering of men and women.

We took our seats in a pew, from which we had an excellent view of the presiding minister. He was a tall, thin, dignified, quiet-looking man. At the first glance one might have expected an orthodox, prosy, soporific sermon, but a more careful inspection of the man revealed a pair of keen, bead-like eyes, which seemed to "take in" every man or woman present in a most unusual manner; tightly compressed lips, and fingers that spasmodically clutched the book they held.

"He doesn't look sensational," I whispered conclusively to my husband.

"He looks very sensational," was the reply.

The preliminary service was a short one, and at the close of a hymn, exquisitely sung, suddenly looking up I saw the minister in the pulpit ready to begin. He made none of those prefatory announcements which are death to the artistic impressiveness of a sermon. Standing in his pulpit, he waited till the last deliciously tuneful strain of the choir had died away, and then gave out his text, clearly and deliberately. Before he had reached the end of the text, he had rivetted my attention, and during the entire sermon I listened to him spell-bound, unconscious of my surroundings.

This was the text:

> "Then the Lord rained upon Sodom and upon Gomorrah brimstone and fire from the Lord out of Heaven;
>
> "And he overthrew those cities, and all the plain, and all the inhabitants of the cities, and that which grew upon the ground.
>
> "And he (Abraham) looked towards Sodom and Gomorrah, and toward all the land of the plain, and beheld, and lo, the smoke of the country went up as the smoke of a furnace."[1]

---

1   Genesis 19:24-25, 28.

He spoke of the optimists who flatter themselves that the sins of the earlier ages are unknown to-day; who believe that civilization has dealt out death to the evils that corrupted a younger world. He tried to show that optimism was the natural sequence of ignorance; that all sin was the result of human weakness, inherited, or by some physiological freak, innate; that there was not a solitary vice recorded in the times gone by that did not exist to-day, magnified and multiplied. Sin could take no new shape, and no one could assert after a careful study of humanity, that it had forgotten any of its old forms. Men were the same now as they were when we first heard of them. Their lives, shortened slightly perhaps by civilization, were identical; their death as inevitable; their physical sufferings synonymous; their joys similar.

He alluded to those who knew of the existence of hateful sins, and who from misplaced scruple, failed to mention them.

"Do not call me illogical," he said, "I do not believe that sin could be abolished by all the sermons in the world. But at least it should be diligently pointed out that it may not gather increased victims. Its spread can be avoided; its contagion diminished. Men will sin as long as the world exists; but many sin voluntarily, won over by those with whom vice is natural."

The pessimism of the sermon frightened me. With him there was no hope of eradicating evil; merely of lessening its influence upon those with whom it was forced to come in contact. It was a very deep, obtuse lecture—too deep for me, I am afraid. I did not understand it thoroughly, though its gist was perfectly clear to me. The methods of the man would have attracted attention anywhere, but I never want to hear another such sermon. I do not believe it could do good. People do not want to be thrilled on Sunday. They need to be comforted and taught to hope for the best. As his last words were uttered, and the congregation, which had listened breathlessly, eagerly, to every word, watched the speaker descend from his pulpit, I looked for the first time since the beginning of the discourse at my husband.

His face was as white as death. His eyes, widely open, were staring fixedly at the pulpit, which was now empty, as though he expected further utterances. His hands hung limp and nerveless at his side.

I touched his arm. He started violently, and turned a face from which every expression of good-fellowship, trust and hope seemed to have fled.

"Arthur," I said, seriously alarmed, "what is the matter? Are you ill? Don't—don't look at me like that."

He tried to smile.

"I wonder if he has delivered that lecture before," he said huskily.

His strange tone surprised me—accustomed as I was, by this time, to surprise.

"Probably not," I said. "Popular preachers, as a rule, do not deliver old sermons, I should think,—for their own sakes."

"Let us go home," he said. "I can't sit through the rest of the service."

As we were going out Arthur asked one of the ushers anxiously if the Doctor were going to speak again that night. The usher smiled.

"No," he said. "One lecture is all he can manage. He exhausts himself. He's as weak as a rat after one of his talks."

My ideas upon the weakness of rats being decidedly limited, I could only infer from the context that it was extreme. We passed out into the street.

"I did not want to hear him again," said Arthur presently, as we walked homewards, "but if he had spoken to-night I feel I must have gone. What an awful sermon!"

"It was indeed," I assented, "we are surely not such hopeless cases as that man wants to make out."

"Do you think so?" he asked.

I looked at him, wondering.

"I am sure of it," I said, with the beautiful certainty of one who never studies any question except upon the surface.

"You are a dear little girl," he said suddenly, with what I considered absolute irrelevance, "and I would believe you rather than—than him. Let us go home and talk. Do you know, dear, I am beginning to feel so happy in your society—No, no" (hastily), "not as I used to be, Elsie. You are doing so much good. I bless the day when we left London."

I looked up at him gladly; could any words have been sweeter than these to me? I doubt it.

CHAPTER 22

W E dined with the multitude that afternoon, and I was glad of it. Arthur was feverishly uneasy. He seemed unable to forget the sermon he had heard in the morning, though why it should have affected him so painfully, I could not exactly understand. Of course I supposed he felt remorse for that part of his life—of our lives—which had brought us to this far off country, and exiled us on its hospitable shores.

Women are not uncharitable, say what you will. I was anxious that my husband should suffer no more for those misdeeds which, it seemed to me, had been so thoroughly left to the past. I wanted him to forget them. I was trying to forget them myself. I flattered myself that my most sanguine hopes would be realized, and that we should return to England as warmly devoted a couple as readers could ever hope to consign to "living happily" ever after.

I was on "pins and needles" lest the subject of the popular preacher should be broached at the dinner-table. There was one old bore present, whom I had seen at the church, and as I knew he was a person with a distinct desire to talk upon the least provocation, I dreaded any opportunity occurring for an outbreak on his part. No one else appeared to have attended divine service that morning, thank goodness! The conversation was beautifully secular, referring to the stage, for the most part.

I had hard work to keep the guests to that subject, but I succeeded. I asked fifty idiotic questions, in the answers to which I had not the faintest interest, beyond the fact that they took up considerable time. I caught the eye of the bore, as I mentally christened him, angrily fixed upon me. He was waiting his opportunity to talk preacher. I knew that. I was determined to prevent his attacking the subject, and I was successful. When I felt a pause coming, I had another question ready to fling broadcast at any one who chose to answer it. I was unfailing in my efforts.

When we finally rose from the table, I cast a look of triumph at the poor old fellow opposite to me. He was biting his stubbly moustache to hide his mortification. He had not been allowed to put in a word edgeways, and he was keenly miserable.

"Was I not thirsty for information, Arthur?" I asked my husband, as he settled himself in our mutual parlor to read the paper, a task with which our church-going had interfered.

"Horribly so," he said, laughing. He seemed to have somewhat recovered himself, though his face was still flushed, and I could see that his hands shook slightly as he held the paper. "What induced you to talk so much, Elsie?"

Oh, men are obtuse beings! He had no idea that my conversational efforts were merely made to spare him pain.

"I had nothing else to do," I answered flippantly. "And I thought my voice sounded well to-day; then, you know, it was Sunday, and I wanted to give them all a treat. Do you see?"

He laughed again. "Elsie," he said, "sometimes I wonder, after listening to your speeches, how it is that you really have depth after all. People who never heard anything but your small talk would think you were good for nothing else."

"Do you think that?" I asked, trying not to appear anxious.

"No, Elsie. Indeed I do not." He glanced at me lovingly. There was a look in his eyes that I had never seen there before. I dropped mine in embarrassment. "I am only thankful—yes, thankful from the bottom of my heart—that you can still be the same little girl as before, after—after what you have endured, since our—our marriage. No, Elsie—" as I made a gesture of disapproval—"there is no reason why we should not discuss the past now, because—because—"

"Because?" I asked breathlessly.

"Because it is losing its interest for me, I am sure," he said in a low tone.

I felt convinced that he spoke the truth. I was confident that no rival supplanted me now, and I saw no harm in congratulating myself already upon the success of my plan. That evening I was in an unusually hilarious mood. I saw success before me in large shining letters. Imperceptibly my manner changed, from that of the love-sick girl, yearning for one kind word from the man upon whom she has lavished all her affection, to the half arrogant self-consciousness of the woman who knows her power. The fool that I was! Great heavens! That such a thing as feminine coquetry should ever be spoken of as charming!

I talked so much nonsense, chatted away so incessantly, and put such a decided veto upon any serious conversation, that Arthur looked at me reproachfully. Surely I had won the right to be gay, I told myself. It had not been often that I had been able to indulge in any frivolity.

"One would think you were on wires to-night, Elsie," said Arthur, in a tone of gentle protest, as after having fluttered all around the room, I sat down beside him.

He took my hand. It was the first time he had ever voluntarily done so. Months ago I would have given years of my life for that little endearment. My heart beat violently as his burning fingers closed over mine; but the devilish spirit of feminine coquetry possessed me; I withdrew my hand abruptly.

"Don't!" I said, rather pettishly.

There was an embarrassing pause; at least it must have been embarrassing for him. I can only think that I was out of my mind that night.

"I suppose when I get back to England," I went on quickly, "that I shall have to set to work and write my impressions of America. Dear me! how extensive they are. Their range is so wide, reaching from this hotel to Central Park, and from Central Park to this hotel. You shall do the editing for me, if you will, and I shall begin as soon as we reach London. Do you consent, Arthur?"

"I cannot think yet of returning to London," he said, almost inaudibly. "I—I—do not want to think of it."

"But you must," I remarked, fanning myself with the newspaper which I had taken from him and folded into a convenient shape. "I am sure neither of us intend to become naturalized Americans, so I don't see why we should remain much longer. I like New York—that is impression No. 1—don't you?"

"I love New York," he said fervently.

"Like the actors and actresses who are interviewed in the newspapers. They all of them seem to love America before they have seen it. I suppose they hope to go home with lots of dollars in their pockets, and want to impress the Americans favorably by liking their country. Don't you think that is a fact, dear?"

I waited for a reply as anxiously as if the question had been one of vital importance.

"Very probably," was the absent rejoinder.

I took up a book and tried to settle down to reading. The letters danced before my eyes, and I flung the book aside with a laugh. I unfolded Arthur's newspaper and gazed stupidly at the advertisements. A dentist offered to extract teeth free of charge, if only the extractee would consent to wear the false article. He had for sale "elegant full gum sets," "gold combination sets," and "platina-lined, porcelain enamelled sets." Of course they were all fearfully cheap. I noted that Mr. John Smith had a two-year-old colt to offer the public for a consideration. It was brown, and had no spots, though it possessed the luxury of a half brother with a record of 2.23; warranted sound. I smiled at the tailor who declared he would make any man a "nobby" suit of clothes for a mere song, and pitied the poor lady who wanted a loan to finish a new house. Poor thing! Why did she begin it, without sufficient money to see the building to its bitter end? I was genuinely interested.

The little clock upon the mantelpiece struck eleven o'clock. How late it was getting! I folded up the newspaper, and sat bolt upright in my chair. I looked at Arthur. His eyes, which seemed to shine like live coals, were fixed upon mine. I crimsoned, for no reason that I can think of.

"It is getting late," I said in a low tone, looking helplessly at the clock.

"Yes."

"We have cooped ourselves up too much to-day," I said, at random. "I wonder why we did not go out this afternoon; the weather was beautiful, and we—we—"

I could not finish the sentence, simply because I did not know what I was going to say when I began it. I sat uneasily listening to the ticking of the clock. It irritated me, and sounded loud as the tramp of soldiers, in the uncomfortable silence that prevailed.

"To-morrow, Arthur," I said, with an effort at levity, as I rose to go, "I shall make you take me for a long walk, as I think it will do us both good. Exercise, you know, is always desirable, and—and—good-night."

I gave him my hand. He took it and, rising, drew me towards him, holding me fondly, firmly in his arms. Bending forward he murmured hoarsely, "Why need we say good-night?"

For one moment I lay quiescent upon his bosom. The next, though my pulses throbbed painfully, and I could feel the hot, feverish blood burning through my veins, I withdrew myself from his clasp, and ran precipitately into my room.

I remained breathless behind the closed door, waiting for him to speak, or at least to let me know that I had not offended him by my abruptness. I waited in vain for five minutes; then I opened my door. He had retired to his room. Looking up at the glass ventilator, I saw that he had put his light out.

In an agony of mortification I retired to my chamber, and throwing myself upon the bed, I cried out against the coquetry inherent in the best of my sex. I had reason to cry out against it.

CHAPTER 23

MY sleep that night was fitful and troubled, and I arose the next morning with a sense of oppression quite unusual with me. Hitherto, when I had retired at night a pessimist, the morning sun invariably brought with it relief, which I believe it is its pleasant mission to do, and I awoke an optimist. But as I dressed on this particular day, I felt uneasy, and anxious without any apparent cause, I told myself.

What had happened to justify this state of mind, I asked? Certainly my wedded life had never looked so promising as it did now. I had won my husband's love, most surely. Could a caprice or two on my part extinguish the flame which I had fanned so long and so diligently? Pshaw! The idea was ridiculous. I was out of sorts. I would not give way to my gloomy thoughts. I would exercise my will, and be happy in spite of myself.

That night Arthur and I were to accompany a charming English couple, whose acquaintance we had made at the hotel, to the opera. It was an appointment dating from a week ago, and I remembered it with regret. I would have preferred passing the evening, alone with my husband. However, I reflected that I could not offend these people, who were of that genial, whole-souled class, whose acquaintance is a privilege, and whose friendship is nothing less than a boon. After all, a future of unoccupied evenings was before me. Arthur and I undoubtedly had time even to grow tired of one another, I thought, and I smiled at the idea.

At that moment an ebony head-waiter knocked at the door and brought in our breakfast, and two minutes later my husband emerged from his chamber, looking bright and pleasant. At all events, I said to myself, if there were any presentiments in the atmosphere, they had all fallen to my share.

"What a lovely day," remarked Arthur, with daring originality as we took our seats at the cosy little round table, and I began to pour out the coffee.

"Yes," I assented, handing him his cup. "After breakfast we are to go for a nice long walk on Broadway to look at the people, and after dinner we are engaged to Mr. and Mrs. Donaldson for the opera."

"You have the programme carefully mapped out," he said, laughing. "Have you been thinking about it long?"

"All night," I said, thoughtlessly.

He looked at me for a moment. My words had no significance, however, other than their literal meaning.

"What do they sing at the opera to-night?" he asked, carelessly.

"Lohengrin."

"I hate Wagner."

"Then you have no right to say so," I assented vigorously, as I dropped an extra piece of sugar into my cup. "If you dare to tell Mr. and Mrs. Donaldson such a thing, the same hotel will never hold us."

He laughed. He was evidently happy this morning. We chatted pleasantly until breakfast was a thing of the past. Then, after having dismissed the morning papers, as was our custom, we started out from the hotel for our walk.

I felt better. My husband's good humor was contagious. It affected me, and I can assure you I was not unwilling to be affected. It was a lovely sunshiny spring day, and Broadway was at its best. It was thronged. Dainty women tripped in and out of the big, well-stocked shops; the beautifully dressed children attracted my attention, and filled me with admiration of juvenile Americans; dapper little men walked quickly by, always in a hurry on general principles. There was a blue sky overhead.

Winter had been successfully vanquished and humanity seemed anxious to celebrate its defeat.

I hummed the one song my mother used to make me sing "before company," when I was at home, and its refrain:

> "The merry, merry sun, the mer-ry sun,
> The merry, merry sun for me-e-e-e."

Then there was a high note at which I had always quaked, and occasionally lowered, much to the anguish of my maternal parent, who liked a good, tuneful shriek, laboring under the impression that it indicated a cultivated voice.

Arthur and I did not talk much, as we were both too intent looking about us to enjoy conversation. The most delightful thing about this walk was that we were not perpetually stopped by a friendly "How d'ye do?" "Fine day," or similar every-day greetings. In London we should have been thus annoyed every five minutes if we had selected Regent Street or Oxford Street, the Broadways of the English metropolis. We were absolutely unnoticed, and it was unspeakably pleasant. I began to think that after all there were worse places than New York in which to make a home.

We were now approaching Madison Square, and I looked around with interest at the lively scene; at the big buildings; the people hurrying about in every direction; the tinkling tram-cars on all sides; the large, lumbering "four-wheelers" jolting over the uneven pavements; the nurses and perambulators just visible on the square; Fifth Avenue stretching far away; the curious, uncomfortable looking omnibusses; and the quaint, Swiss-chalet-like structure marking a station on the elevated railway, to be seen traversing the wide thoroughfare on the left. I was fascinated. We crossed the street and found ourselves in front of an enormous, ponderous, gray hotel. A large portico stretched from the entrance to this building, and afforded a standing place for a score or so of men, apparently bent upon ogling passers-by, who unfortunately could not avoid passing them.

I hate a congregation of men, anywhere, so I walked quickly past this group and stopped before I reached the corner to allow Arthur to come up with me. I turned. He was not by my side. He was standing in front of the portico gazing into the lobby. As I waited, he approached me, and I was startled as I looked at his face.

It was livid, and he was trembling violently.

"I am ill, Elsie," he said, quickly. "I must be ill. Perhaps it is my heart. I—I think so. Let us go home."

He looked ill indeed. I told myself that it must be heart trouble, as a few moments before he had been perfectly well, and there was nothing else I could think of to affect him in that manner. We returned to the hotel, and I insisted upon sending for a doctor. Arthur rebelled, but I would not give way. The Doctor declared that there was nothing at all the matter with Arthur's heart. It was sound. He thought his system was out of order generally, and wrote out a prescription. In fact he did what most doctors do, in the usual pompous, would-be impressive way.

"I am going to send down word to Mrs. Donaldson," I said, half an hour later, "that we cannot accompany her to the Opera to-night. I can't say I'm particularly sorry," I added, carelessly.

Arthur started up quickly from the sofa upon which he had been reclining. "You must go," he declared, "there is no reason why you should not do so. Do not offend these people, Elsie. We have found them very pleasant acquaintances, and I believe they are only going to accommodate us."

I looked at him in amazement. His eagerness was almost painful to see; there was a bright red spot upon each cheek, and his eyes shone fiercely. His gentle, sympathetic manner of the past few days seemed to have disappeared.

"If you insist upon my going," I said, to humor him, "I will go; but I would sooner stay at home with you."

"Nonsense." He spoke so roughly that the tears started to my eyes. He saw this and looked remorseful.

"I will follow you, Elsie, if I can," he said. "Perhaps I m-may join you during the evening, though—"

He got no farther. He was ill, I thought, and possibly an evening alone would do him good. I had given him no opportunities to miss me since we had been in America. I had found so much pleasure in his society, that I was determined to enjoy it. Did I not know, clearly enough, that he loved me, at last? Had I not been able to recognize that fact with sufficient distinctness? Of course I had. He wanted me to go to the opera, and I would go and amuse myself. I should be able to think of him waiting for me at home, and growing perhaps miserably lonely in my absence. He would possibly tell me when I returned that he could not spare me again, and then how thoroughly happy I should feel! Perhaps, after all, Arthur's indisposition was for the best. I felt that it might be, and my spirits, which had been rapidly sinking since my return from our walk, rose with considerable energy.

We dined in the big dining-room, Arthur declaring that he was not ill enough to be treated as an invalid, and after that meal I robed myself in gorgeous apparel. Arthur walked up and down the parlor, and through my closed door I could hear his quick uneven footsteps. I was soon ready, and my husband wrapped me up in my *sortie de bal.*

"Good-night, dear," I said briskly.

"Good-night."

"Are you not going to kiss me?" I asked, reproachfully, as he took my hand, and let it drop rather coldly, evidently inclined to make this do duty as a farewell salutation.

He bent over me in silence, and pressed his lips to my upturned face. The kiss chilled me. It reminded me of the first he had ever given me, and I shuddered slightly. For one moment a great feeling of disappointment came over me; the next brought with it the remembrance of last night, and my anxiety was swept away as by a consuming flame.

I ran lightly down stairs and joined the genial Donaldsons. They were waiting for me in the parlors. When I saw Mrs. Donaldson, I really felt pleased that my husband was absent. She was *décolletée*[1] in a way that made my cheeks burn. The strip of satin that, for politeness' sake she called a bodice, was so bewilderingly narrow, that one had to look for it carefully, in order to find it. She was a nice little woman, this Mrs. Donaldson. I liked what I knew of her, but I had no desire to know quite as much as her attire revealed.

"How charming you look," she said as I entered the room, and turned my eyes away from her chubby beauty, "and what a bright color you have in your cheeks. One might almost suspect rouge," she added, laughing.

The bright color was all on her account. I have no doubt it looked very pleasing, but I knew it would not remain. I was one of those unfortunate

---

1   Displaying a plunging neckline.

girls who rarely look rosy unless they are blushing or suffering from indigestion.

Mr. Donaldson was delighted with his wife. To him she was a perpetual source of pleasing astonishment. He saw nothing improper in her costume—or rather want of costume—and I am quite convinced that if she had set forth for the Opera, attired in a sweet smile and a tunic, he would have been satisfied. I reflected that there would probably be other women as outrageously clad as my friend, and reconciled myself in this manner to being seen with her.

I was right. In the vast Opera House the display of feminine undress was so startling, that it took my breath away. It was ten times worse than anything I had ever seen in London. I had been told that New York was, in many respects, an exaggeration of London, and I felt I could believe it.

"Lohengrin," as I had already said, was the opera; not that it mattered much. The occupants of the boxes paid very little attention to what was going on upon the stage. They talked and laughed and recognized one another; opera-glassed the other side of the house, and commented upon each new arrival within range of their vision. It was a lively scene, at any rate.

Mr. and Mrs. Donaldson pretended to be very fond of Wagner, and I believe they imagined that they were. Being strangers in the city they had few friends to recognize, and were tolerably interested in the opera. Mrs. Donaldson's costume proved to be positively prudish. There were others that were so much more astonishing, that I felt quite sorry for her. She had started out prepared to astonish the natives, and lo! it was the natives who were astonishing her.

I treasured up a few descriptions with which to regale Arthur when I went home. I imagined I heard his hearty laugh, and that phrase of his, "Your speeches always amuse me so, Elsie."

Dear old man! How pleasant the future looked, stretched out before us! What happiness there seemed to be held in store for us by coming years.

I looked at Mrs. Donaldson. She was yawning desperately, and seemed vexed to be caught in the act.

"It is not a good performance, by any means," she said to justify herself. I agreed with her. I was anxious to go home. Arthur had not joined us, and I had heard all the Wagner I wanted for this evening. I tried to delicately insinuate to Mrs. Donaldson that it would be advisable to leave early and avoid the crush. She would not hear of this, however, and favored me with such a Medusa-like stare, that I was silenced most effectually.

The opera was over at last, and slowly and solemnly we wound our way down the broad, red-carpeted staircase. A carriage was awaiting us and we were soon rolling hotelward. On the whole I was rather glad I had accompanied the Donaldsons. The scene at the Opera House had amused me somewhat, and I had plenty to say to Arthur, which was in itself a boon. As my husband was not sentimental, and I was determined to be as prosaic as possible, a few novelties to be added to our conversational stock would not be amiss. I wondered if the evening had seemed very long to him. I felt he would not like to admit that it had, but I was resolved that my object should be to force him to make that confession. I pictured him seated in the arm-chair reading and waiting for me—especially waiting.

I said good-night to the Donaldsons as soon as we arrived at the hotel, and resisted their invitation to supper. Supper indeed! Going quietly upstairs I coyly knocked at the parlor door, and then drawing back into the shadow, waited for it to be opened. There was no answer. In my coyness, I supposed I had not made myself heard, so with decidedly more energy, I knocked again.

It was long past midnight. Arthur must have fallen asleep, I reflected. He was tired, and such a vigil was by no means encouraging. So I turned the knob of the door and walked in.

The gas was burning brightly; there was an untidy gathering of newspapers upon the sofa, and the room had all the appearance of an extremely occupied apartment. Arthur was not there, however. With a little sob of utter disappointment, I told myself that he had not waited up for me. Oh! how unkind of him, when he knew how much I should have appreciated that little act of attention! In his place, I would have remained awake all night. Pshaw! What peculiar creatures men were, I thought. Their ideas were so absolutely opposed to ours that it was wonderful such a thing as a matrimonial partnership could ever exist for any length of time. Then I stopped in my mental deliberations to remember that I had left Arthur avowedly indisposed. How could I tell that he had not been taken worse during the evening? Surely it was my duty to ascertain the facts of the case. I felt a qualm of remorse as I saw how ready I was to place my husband in the wrong.

I went to the door of his bed-room and knocked. There was no answer.

Becoming seriously alarmed, I knocked again; this time loudly, with the same result. Then, resolved to stand upon no ceremony, I opened the door and walked into his room. It was in complete darkness. A cold apprehension of trouble seized me, and I shivered violently. I went to the table where I knew he kept his matches, and with trembling fingers drew one from the box. I dreaded to light it. I struck the match, however, and closed my eyes for a second. When I had summoned up courage to look around me, I saw that the room was empty. The bed had not been occupied, and my husband's coats had disappeared from their hooks in the closet, as I could see through its open door. My knees shook, and I almost fell, as I saw that his trunk and valise had also gone.

For a moment I was too dazed to realize what all this meant. I sat down upon the bed, and held my hands to my forehead, which was throbbing so vigorously that it almost deadened the recognition of any other fact. Arthur had gone and taken his trunk with him. He had left me without a word of explanation. I sprang up, rushed from the room, and started down stairs to see the hotel clerk and ask him if my husband had left any message with him. I dreaded to face the man at such an hour, and then I suddenly remembered that the clerk who had been on duty before midnight had undoubtedly been succeeded by this time.

I ran back to my rooms. The perspiration was dripping from my forehead and the glimpse I caught of my ghastly face in the looking-glass, which hung above the mantelpiece, frightened me. Ah! there was an envelope in the frame of this looking-glass, which was evidently meant to attract my attention. I made a bound forward and seized it. It was addressed simply to "Elsie."

A cry escaped my lips as I saw this. He had left me, and this was his explanation. The letters on the envelope became enveloped in a blurred mist, and I could see nothing. I steadied myself by grasping the mantelpiece with one hand, while I pressed the other, holding the letter, against my heart. I must have stood thus for a minute; then, with a feeling of astonishment at my own helplessness, I broke open the envelope and read this, written in a trembling, hurried hand, mis-spelt and blotted:

"Elsie:

"No one will ever know how I have tried to obliterate the memory of a sinful past, and make you the husband, which—noble girl that you are—you deserve. I have long recognized the fact that the old miserable ideas which we have discussed so often, and which led to our marriage, were impossible. I say I have tried to become a good, manly husband to you. I thought I had succeeded until this morning, and so did you, poor girl, but it seems we were both mistaken. I am a wretch. Forget me. Return to England with the Donaldsons next week. I shall come to you no more. After this final step, it would of course be impossible. I make no excuses for myself. I am not worth any, and no one recognizes that fact more than,

"Arthur Ravener"

The room seemed to be revolving. An awful giddiness overwhelmed me, and I fell heavily to the floor.

CHAPTER 24

I DO not know how I passed that awful night. I have a dim recollection of sitting up in hopeless dejection, on the sofa, conscious only of my intense longing for daylight. I could do nothing while darkness reigned; in fact I was absolutely helpless. I could only hope that the darkness which rendered me powerless to act, would have the same effect upon my husband. I could understand nothing. I seemed to be dazed. Not an idea of the truth dawned upon me. Our relations had been so pleasant; I was just about to attain the object of my visit to America, when, in the most inexplicable manner, my husband had left me. As I look back now I wonder how I could have been so dense. It appears to me now that the veriest blockhead could have grasped the situation.

At seven o'clock I sent for the hotel clerk, and asked him if he could tell me anything about my husband's departure from the hotel. In his suave, horribly superior manner, he informed me that he had not been on duty, and the "gentleman" who had been in charge of the desk before midnight, would not be "around" again until noon. I was in despair. I told this fat, oily official that it was really a matter of life and death with me. If he would only send for the clerk who had last seen my husband, I would pay liberally for the trouble I gave. This, and this alone, seemed to invest the case with interest for him. He promised to send for the day clerk, and in a short time I found him in my room. He could tell me very little. At about nine o'clock Mr. Ravener had ordered a carriage, and had taken a small trunk and a valise with him. He had not said where he was going, or anything concerning his return.

I begged the clerk to send for the man who had driven Mr. Ravener from the hotel. He looked with gentle surprise at my distress, as though it were extremely incomprehensible to him. Arthur had left with the few lines he had written me, money to the amount of five hundred pounds, and I tipped the clerk recklessly. He was thereupon much impressed with my case, and promised to do all he could to help me.

The driver was a big, burly fellow, with a red nose, and a florid, bulldog face. My heart sank when I saw him. Heaven help all who have to depend upon so sottish a class of people for important information. He had great trouble in remembering the fact that he had taken anybody from the hotel at nine o'clock the evening before.

"Think! think! man," I cried frantically. "If you will remember everything, and tell me what I want to know, I'll give you this."

I held up a ten-dollar bill before him, and his eyes flashed with eager desire through the heavy, drunken film that covered them, as he saw the money. He sat down, stopped chewing the tobacco which he had been masticating vigorously and attempted to think, with a brutish effort. Then he referred to a little book that he carried in his pocket, and in a few minutes a ray of something distantly related to intelligence lighted up his features.

"The gen'lman told me ter take him to the big marble building on the corner o' Twen'y-third Street and Broadway," said he stolidly. "He said he guessed it was an hotel, and I said I guessed he meant the Fifth Avenue. When we got there, a man come to the carriage and helped him out. I guess the man was expectin' him. No, I didn't hear what they says. A porter come up and took the gen'lman's baggage. He give me a five dollar bill, and told me not to wait. That's all I know, mum."

"What kind of a man met Mr. Ravener at the hotel?" I exclaimed, gasping, with a terrible fear upon me.

"I dunno, mum," was the answer. "A ordinary, every-day gen'lman, he seemed to me. He was rather stout, I think, but I didn't pay no partickler attention to him, mum. I ain't in the habit of lookin' at every man I meet so as I can give a description of him afterwards, mum."

"Was Mr. Ravener's baggage taken upstairs?" I asked, trying to speak calmly.

"I dunno, mum. Ye see when I got my fare I just skipped. T'wasn't no good my waitin' around."

"All right—now go," I said hurriedly. "Here's the money."

I wanted to be alone. I dismissed the hotel clerk, and began to dress quickly. I would go to the Fifth Avenue Hotel at once. I should doubtless find Arthur there. I absolutely declined to think at all until I could solve the case. I would not torture my mind by imagining this, and suspecting that. I would, if possible, deal with facts only. I had no difficulty in keeping my mind a blank. I was bewildered by the magnitude of the misfortune that had fallen upon me in a strange country. I was soon ready to start, and ordering a carriage, I told the driver to take me to the Fifth Avenue Hotel, and wait for me there.

No sooner had I arrived at the hotel, than quick as a flash of lightning, a great deal of what had been inexplicable lay solved before me. This was the big building that Arthur and I had passed the preceding day. I remembered the crowd of men standing under the porch, and the annoyance I felt at being ogled. I had walked alone to the corner of the street, and, turning, had beheld Arthur gazing in at the lobby. His livid face had filled me with alarm, and he had declared that he was ill. That night he had been driven to this hotel. The reason was too clear for even a blind fool like myself to fail to understand. He had seen some one in the lobby—some one whom he had not expected to see. I could not doubt who it was—no, I could not doubt it, though I would have given all I possessed to be able to do so.

I walked into the hotel, elbowing my way through a crowd of wide-staring men, and went at once to the clerk. I asked him if a young man named Arthur Ravener had arrived at the hotel the previous night. He referred to his register, but could find no such name. I told him he must be mistaken, but this had the effect of rendering him mute. I forgot that an American hotel clerk could not possibly, under any circumstances, be mistaken. I then informed him that I had just spoken with the driver who had conducted Mr. Ravener, with his baggage, to the hotel, and left him there. He was surprised, but he had not been "on duty" at that time.

He suggested that I speak to Mr. Price, the detective of the hotel, who was always in the lobby, and whose keen eyes saw everybody who came in and who went out.

I found this detective courteous, well-informed, and remarkably intelligent. I explained my case to him.

"Last night," he said, "shortly after nine o'clock, a carriage drove up to the hotel. It contained a young man, and I noticed that his face was deathly white. In fact, it was this circumstance that interested me at first. This ghastly hue could not have been normal with any living being. Before he had time to leave the carriage, a fellow, of whom I will speak presently, rushed out and opened the door. He called to a porter, and after having dismissed the carriage, ordered that the trunk and valise which the gentleman with the white face brought, be sent to the dock of the Guion line of steamers, with his own."

I uttered an exclamation of horror, and the detective stopped in alarm. "Go on," I cried.

"The two then went upstairs. The young man seemed to be much excited. He could hardly reply to the glib remarks of his companion. He appeared to be in a dream. I suspected that there was something strange about this, Madame," said Mr. Price, safely, "but I did not see on what ground I could interfere. The gentleman who met your—your—husband?—arrived from England about three days ago. He brought a big black trunk, labelled conspicuously "J. D.," while he registered under the name of Frank Clarke. A leather pocket-book was found in the hotel the other day. It contained a large sum of money. Mr. Clarke claimed it, and declared that it belonged to him, although the name on the cards which were in it was—"

"What?" I asked breathlessly, although I knew full well.

Mr. Price drew a slip of paper from his pocket. "The name was Jack Dillington," he said. "Captain Jack Dillington. I was very suspicious when he claimed this pocket-book. He was able to tell me exactly its contents. He explained that the cards belonged to a friend, and I had to believe him."

"Although you saw his trunk marked 'J. D.'?" I asked impatiently.

"Yes," replied the detective. "I had my suspicions, but what could I do? A man can travel under any name he likes; we may suspect that he is doing so for some improper purpose, but unless he does something which justifies our suspicions, I am afraid we could not make out a case. Mr. Clarke, or Dillington, behaved himself properly. I was not asked to watch him. I could not suppose that he—he—"

"Was running away with a woman's husband," I said, wearily. Fate seemed to be against me. I felt it was useless to struggle.

"Exactly," he assented, looking at me keenly.

"I am much obliged to you for having told me all that you know," I said, in the same tired way. He bowed, and I went out to my carriage. I told the driver to take me to the Guion line dock.

It was not much use, though I thought I might as well drain my cup misery to the dregs. I saw it all. Arthur had told Captain Dillington of our proposed trip to America. I remembered the day when I had gone to his room and found the door locked. I called to mind the sudden shutting the window which I had unmistakably heard. Captain Dillington had probably consented to this departure, and the fool whom I had married had not suspected that he would be followed. Consequently, when by mere chance Arthur had seen Dillington in the lobby of the Fifth Avenue Hotel, he had been astounded. The horrible influence which this man exerted over the weaker vessel must have been all-powerful. It had in one moment knocked away the barriers which in weeks of perseverance I had raised. I had been right in one respect. It was only by removing him from this man, whom I felt to be his evil genius, that I could have hoped to win my husband.

For the first time I began to doubt if there were a "woman in the case," after all. But the doubt brought no relief to my mind. I almost wished that I could have known that my husband was on his way to some woman who loved him well, even if unwisely. As it was, I could only suppose that the Captain's evil influence was exerted over Arthur for some object that I could not guess at, though I felt sure it must be wicked, and to be feared.

At the Guion dock, I learned that the Alaska had sailed for Liverpool at six o'clock that morning. I had no difficulty in ascertaining that two gentlemen had driven up about ten minutes before the vessel sailed. One of then was stout; the other slight and with a pale face.

I almost laughed at the completeness with which one piece of evidence fitted into the other.

I drove back to my hotel. I was alone in a strange country, but it was not that fact which annoyed me. No one would run away with me, I was sorry to say. I thought of the future, and it seemed so black that I could not look into it.

I resolved to make one more effort to save my husband from a fate which I did not understand. I saw that a Cunard steamer was sailing the next day—the fast Etruria. I could reach Liverpool before the Alaska.

I had no sooner seen this than one last ray of hope roused me to energy. I packed up my few goods, and the next day I was speeding across the ocean.

I have little more to say. I arrived in Liverpool, as I thought I should do, a day before the Alaska. I put up at the Adelphi Hotel, and gave orders that as soon as the Alaska was sighted I should be notified. I went down to the dock in due course. I watched the crowd of cabin passengers alight from the tender, but my husband and his accomplice were not to be found. Later, I learned that several passengers had landed at Queenstown, and I could not doubt but that they had been among them. They had probably suspected that I might follow on a fast Cunarder, and had rightly thought that I should not stop at Queenstown.

Well, they had won the battle, and if two men could find any glory in having vanquished one weak woman, let them find and keep it, I said to myself bitterly.

I was defeated and heart-broken. I returned to the house in Kew, "wound up" my affairs there—as they say in the mercantile world—and went abroad, in seclusion.

CHAPTER 25

A GRAVE scandal was agitating the never very placid surface of Parisian society, and causing an immense sensation in the French metropolis. Men of high standing were involved, and names that had hitherto stood in lofty superiority, were mentioned in connection with one of the most disgraceful revelations that Paris had known in many years. The newspapers might possibly have ignored the affair as much as possible on account of the nauseating nature of the details, but this course could not be pursued. The names of the malefactors were too well known and too prominent. The people demanded that the details be made public, and when the reputable journals maintained a silence upon the matter, they transferred their allegiance to one or two disreputable papers that dealt with scandal without gloves. It was evident that the case must be ventilated, and bowing to the inevitable, each journal took it up. Everybody knows that the French papers are none too nice, so it will be readily understood that happenings bad enough for them to endeavor to suppress must indeed have been bad.

The London papers devoted a great deal of space to the scandal; in fact they seemed to gloat over it, and when it was subsequently hinted that the contagion had spread to the English metropolis, Londoners grew more and more interested each day.

"We know of no spectacle so ridiculous as the British public in one of its periodical fits of morality," says Macaulay.[1] "In general, elopements, divorces, and family quarrels pass with little notice. We read the scandal, talk about it for a day, and forget it. But once in six or seven years, our virtue becomes outrageous."

It seemed as though this "once in six or seven years" had come.

I was in London at the time of which I write, brought from the seclusion into which I had withdrawn, by business connected prosaically with my financial affairs, and requiring my presence. For two years I had been trying to live down the memory of the events that had wrecked my life. I had not seen my husband since the night I had left him to go to the opera. We were still bound by the ties of matrimony. My friends had suggested divorce, but I dreaded the publicity of the courts, and, after all, why should I suffer it? The tie that bound me was not irksome, since he, to whom I was bound, left me to my own resources.

One afternoon, shortly after my arrival in London, I picked up the *Daily Telegraph*, more in idleness than in curiosity. Of course I had heard about the scandal which seemed to be dragging London and Paris into a cesspool of vice. The journal in question was particularly sensational on the day in question. In spite of myself, I was compelled to read. I had not gone far, before I was startled into painful interest. One of the ringleaders of the evil-doers had been arrested at Newhaven, where he had just landed from Dieppe and Paris. He had made a full confession, and the London police had seized upon it with avidity. He declared that there were many Londoners in Paris at the present time, who were deeply involved in the matter. The principal of these, he said, was a man who was passing under the assumed name of Delácroix. He was an Englishman whose real name was Dillington.

I uttered a cry as this name, fraught with such bitter recollections for me, was thus brought to my attention. For two years, I had neither heard nor seen it, and now, in cold type, it stood before me. I could

---

1   Thomas Babington Macaulay (1800-1859), British writer, reviewer, and politician. The lines appear in Macaulay's 1830 review "On Moore's Life of Lord Byron."

not doubt that the Dillington mentioned, was the one who had been instrumental in destroying my happiness. The article went on to say that he was staying at present at a little hostelry known as the Hotel Vaupin, in the Rue Geoffroy-Marie.

I rose with an impulse of overwhelming force upon me. Dillington at the Hotel Vaupin; my husband must be there too. Yes, he was still my husband in the eyes of God and man, and he must be saved while there was yet time. The thought of his danger swept away for the moment all memories of the bitter wrongs I had suffered at his hands. They faded from my mind as though they had not existed. I saw him only as he was that night when he had asked me why I need leave him, and I, impelled by a fatal feminine coquetry, had rushed away, leaving his passionate question unanswered. Perhaps I might have saved him then if—no, it would not bear thinking about. I would go to his assistance at once, flinging all conventionalities to the winds.

I hastily packed a small valise, ordered a hansom, and one hour after I had become acquainted with the *Telegraph* article, I was on my way to the Charing Cross Station. I was not afraid of meeting anybody, as I had been on a former journey, also taken in the interests of my miserable marriage. I did not care who saw me, and yet, as though to contradict this mental avowal, I gave a sigh of relief as I found the railway carriage, which took me to Folkestone, unoccupied.

I arrived in Paris early the following morning, before the sleepy officials at the Gare du Nord seemed to have shaken off their slumbers. I had no time to think of putting up at any hotel; speed was a question of life and death with me; so summoning a *fiacre*,[1] I had my valise put inside, and told the driver to take me to the Hotel Vaupin. He had never heard of it, he said. I started, surprised that a man like Captain Dillington, whose ideas I had always thought were of the most extravagant, could be found at an hotel unknown to a station cab driver. I told the man that the Vaupin was in the Rue Geoffroy-Marie, and then it was his turn to stare. I urged him to hurry, and he did so, seemingly under protest. Down the interminable Rue de Lafayette we went. It had just begun its day's life, and the last of the *chiffoniers*[2] was seen vanishing as

---

1   Hackney-coach.
2   Ragpickers.

though he could not stand the glare of the morning. Soon we turned into the Rue de Trevise; then, crossing the Rue Richer, we entered the Rue Geoffroy-Marie.

It is a narrow, dirty little street, in the centre of the commerce of Paris. The Hotel Vaupin had a conspicuous gilt sign in front of it; the driver drew up, and opening the door of the carriage, assisted me to alight. I told him to wait for me, as I had no idea of remaining in the semi-squalor of this locality very long. He eyed me suspiciously, and said he would wait, but he would like to be paid for the trip we had already made. Angry, even at this delay, I paid him, and passed at once into the hotel.

The proprietor was a big, burly, flaxen-haired fellow, phlegmatic, yet still a Frenchman. He came to the door to meet me. I hesitated for a moment, and then asked:

"Is M. Delacroix in?"

He looked at me keenly, and did not answer at once. "Does Madame not know?" he asked, haltingly.

"Know what?" I demanded, with a sinking heart.

"M. Delacroix was arrested this morning," said the proprietor, "at my hotel, too—alas! that I should tell it. He is charged with being involved in these—in these scandals, and—"

He went on in an affably recitative manner, but I heard no more. What a fool I had been to imagine that the French authorities would ignore the confession that I had read in the *Telegraph*. They had acted upon it at once. It had probably been known to them before the *Telegraph* had gone to press.

"Was M. Delacroix alone at this hotel?" I asked breathlessly. The proprietor seemed to be taken aback at my excitement—for a moment only, however.

"M. Delacroix came to this house some weeks ago," he said. "He was accompanied by a young gentleman, *un charmant garçon*,[1] who occupied a room adjoining his, and—"

"Go on," I cried, frantically.

"He is still here."

"Ah!" This exclamation escaped me; I could not help giving it utterance. "I will go up to his room," I said, trying to quiet my throbbing pulses.

---

1   A charming boy.

I felt that I could not move. Now that I knew Arthur was here, I hated to see him; to confess, by this interview, that I understood his unhappy life. I made a mighty effort, however, and was ready, when the proprietor told me that the apartment was the first room to the right, on the second floor, to seek it.

I slowly ascended the uneven, miserably carpeted staircase. Not a soul did I meet. If there were any other occupants than Arthur in the hotel, they kept themselves out of sight. I stopped in front of room No. 18. It was the first to the right on the second floor. I knocked at the door, but received no answer. I listened, but nobody seemed to be behind the thin, cracked door to which a lock and key offered but slight security. I repeated my knocks without the least success, and, at last, I retraced my steps, found the proprietor, and told him that he must be mistaken; that the young Englishman must be out.

"No, he is not out," said the man vigorously. "I have stood here all day, I wished to warn him," hesitatingly, "for—for I liked him. He has not left his room. I can swear to that. Come with me; I think I can make him hear."

Oppressed by the awful character of the events in which I seemed myself to be involved, I followed him, and again ascended the creaking staircase. The proprietor's emphatic knock was as unsuccessful as mine. He waited for a minute or two, and then opening the door of the room next to No. 18, which he told me had been occupied by M. Delacroix, he entered that apartment. He tried a door inside, connecting the two rooms. It was locked.

There was a strange look upon his face as he came out. "I will break open the door," he said.

The task was not a hard one. An application of his big shoulder to the frail portal; a not very powerful push, and the lock gave way. We stood inside the room. It was darkened. The proprietor went to the window and drew up the shabby blinds. As much light as the close proximity of another house would allow struggled into the room. It was in complete disorder. The bed had not been slept in. The floor was littered with books, newspapers and clothes.

I turned, and in an old chintz-covered arm-chair by the fire-place, saw my husband. His face was white, his head was bent slightly forward. He looked as though he had fallen asleep in an uncomfortable position.

"Arthur," I cried, springing forward with a loud cry; but the proprietor, who had been standing by the chair for a minute, came forward and pulled me towards the door.

"He is dead," he said simply.

Dead!

In a dazed way I walked up to the chair and coldly glanced at the face, which, white and expressionless, looked to me unlike that which I had known as my husband's. The proprietor quietly went from the room and left me alone with Arthur. On the mantel-piece my staring eyes saw a small bottle, on which a label marked "laudanum" stood out with fearful clearness. Then I realized it all. With an agonized cry I flung myself into the unresisting arms of my husband, I kissed his cold, dead lips, his face, and the open, unseeing eyes, as I would have kissed him in life, had he willed it so. Ah! he could not ward me off now. He was mine, and I would cherish him forever.

Suddenly I sprang back, a horrible feeling of repulsion creeping over me. Just above Arthur's head, on the wall, I saw two portraits, placed together in a single frame. One represented my husband, happy and smiling; the other showed the hateful features of Captain Dillington. My grief gave place to a violent, overpowering sense of anger. Tearing the frame from the wall, I threw it roughly to the floor. The glass broke with a crisp, short noise; but with my feet I crushed it into atoms. Then stooping down, I picked up the photographs, and tore them into smallest pieces. In the same frenzied manner, I went to the window, opened it, and gathering up the bits of glass—regardless of the fact that they cut my hands until the blood flowed freely—I flung them with the torn photographs from the window and looked from it until I saw them scatter in all directions. Then turning away, and without another look at the dead form in the chair, I left the room and the hotel.

THE END.